HOW TO MAKE
GREAT STUFF
FOR YOUR ROOM

. . . .

written and illustrated by

Mary Wallace

Greey de Pencier Books

How to Make Great Stuff for Your Room

Also available in this series: *How to Make Great Stuff to Wear.*

Books from OWL are published by Greey de Pencier Books, 56 The Esplanade, Suite 302, Toronto, Ontario M5E 1A7.

*OWL and the OWL colophon are trademarks of the Young Naturalist Foundation. Greey de Pencier is a licensed user of trademarks of the Young Naturalist Foundation.

This book was published with the generous support of the Canada Council and the Ontario Arts Council.

Published in Canada by Greey de Pencier Books.
Published simultaneously in the United States by Firefly Books (U.S.) Inc., P.O. Box 1338, Ellicott Station, Buffalo, NY 14205.

Canadian Cataloguing in Publication Data

Wallace, Mary, 1950 –
    How to make great stuff for your room

Includes index.
ISBN 0-920775-85-3

1. Bedrooms – Juvenile literature. 2. Interior decoration – Juvenile literature.
3. Handicraft – Juvenile literature. I. Title.

NK2117.B4W35 1992   j747.7'7   C92-093594-X

Design & Art Direction: Julia Naimska
Photography: Eekhoff & Muir Studio

Crafts on the front cover, clockwise from upper left: Pencil Organizer, Letter Pillows, Person Pillow, Designer Sheets, Headboard Cover, Four-Shoe Footstool.

Crafts on the back cover, clockwise from upper left: Hotdog Pillow, Garbage Gobbler, Painted Chair, Comfy Bed Bolster.

Printed in Hong Kong

A   B   C   D   E   F   G

INTRODUCTION

Your room is your own personal space. With the ideas you'll find in this book, and a little creativity, you can turn your room into a special space with a style that's all your own. You can probably find most of the materials you'll need around home. So, if you want to give your room a jazzy new look, read on.

CONTENTS

You'll find photographs of all this Great Stuff for Your Room on pages 35 to 42.

FURNISHINGS: INTRODUCTION

- Almost everyone's room has furniture, but some pieces of furniture are more fun than others. Take a look at your room. It's probably already furnished, but with a few changes you can add a lot more character. Imagine stretching out on a self-made sausage chair, while gazing at your new hamburger footstool and some other zany furnishings you've created.

- Gather up some odd socks, old shoes, T-shirts, sweatsuits, nylon stockings, yarn and old upholstered cushions. Use an old wire lampshade to give new life to your bedside lamp. Or make some snazzy shelves out of ordinary cardboard boxes. But remember – it's always a good idea to get permission to use these odds and ends before beginning a project.

- Whenever latex paint is called for, use leftover latex housepaint. It's non-toxic, washes out with water when wet, and is waterproof when dry. For other projects, use tempera paints, but cover them with a clear finish such as varnish or acrylic so they won't rub off. If you need fabric paint, look for it at any craft or fabric store. Many department and toy stores sell it, too.

- Squeeze bottles are useful for painting thin lines or detailed patterns. Some paint can be purchased in small squeeze bottles. You can pour other paint into empty plastic squeeze bottles you might have around the house. More squeeze bottles can be obtained from a hairdressing shop.

- Don't forget to plan ahead. Draw chalk lines before you cut or paint – they are easy to erase later and prevent a lot of errors. Make sure that you have a pair of good, sturdy scissors for cutting.

- Keep adults happy by covering your work surface with several layers of newspaper. And don't forget that cleanup is part of every project.

Imagine sleeping in a wooden box with sliding doors that close you in. A few hundred years ago people in England thought that was healthy since it kept out germs and cold drafts. In other times and places, people have slept on beds of straw, hair, felt, feathers and fur. What type of bed would you find comfortable?

Long ago in many parts of the world, if you were an ordinary person, chances are you wouldn't have owned a single chair. You would have sat on a long bench instead. Back then, the first chairs were thrones, which only very important people owned or sat in. These seats probably weren't too comfortable, though — they were usually carved from stone or wood and were not padded.

FOUR-SHOE FOOTSTOOL

Turn a cardboard box and four old shoes into a "fun"tastic footstool.

- **MATERIALS**
  - large bowl • 2 cups flour • 3 cups water
  - ⅔ cup salt • large scissors • medium-size, sturdy cardboard box
  - 4 old shoes (all different styles) • 4 wooden dowels • masking tape • newspaper • extra cardboard
  - sandpaper • several colors of latex housepaint • medium-size paintbrush • small paintbrush

- **PREPARATION**
  - In a large bowl, combine the flour, water and salt. This mixture is your papier-mâché paste. Mix more as you need it.

- **INSTRUCTIONS**
  1. Cut a slit on either side of each lower corner of the cardboard box, as shown. Slip a shoe under each corner of the box and into the slits. Trim off the bottom of each corner so that the box rests on the ground when the shoes are in place.

  2. Ask an adult to help you cut a wooden dowel to fit between each shoe and the inside corner of the box. Fasten each dowel with masking tape. Stuff the shoe openings with crumpled newspaper.

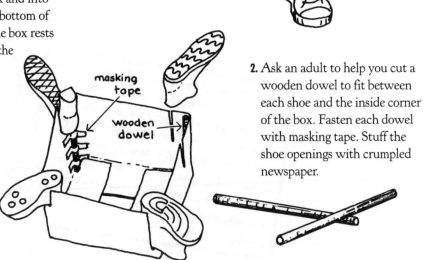

masking tape

wooden dowel

3. Cut two pieces of sturdy cardboard the same size as the top of the box. Glue them onto the box with papier-mâché paste for a smooth surface.

4. Tear the newspaper into strips about 2 inches x 10 inches. Dip the strips, one at a time, into the paste, and pull out between two fingers to remove any excess paste. Secure the four dowels inside the box with three layers of papier-mâché strips.

cardboard

crumpled newspaper

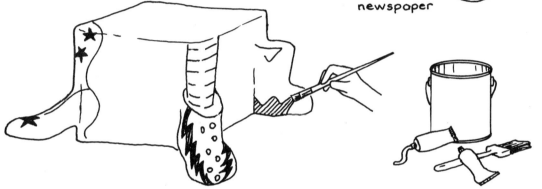

5. Place strips on the footstool form, rubbing them gently to remove air bubbles. Cover the entire footstool with at least three layers of papier-mâché strips. Smooth out any bumps with your fingers.

6. Set the footstool aside for a few days until it is completely dry. Sand any rough edges.

7. Cover your footstool with two coats of paint. Paint a different-style sock and shoe on each corner, adding details with the small paintbrush.

. . . .

● **VARIATION**

● For a matching bedside table, stuff four old gloves with scrunched pieces of newspaper and tape one onto each top corner of a sturdy cardboard box, palm side in and fingers up. Glue three large, cardboard circles on top. Cover the whole table form with three layers of papier-mâché.

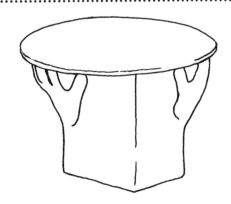

Hamburger Footstool

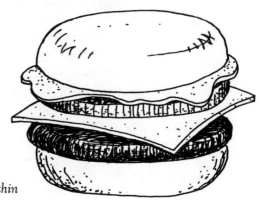

Put together a giant bun, a tomato slice, a lettuce leaf, a cheese slice and a meat patty to make a hilarious hamburger footstool.

- **Materials**
  - 20 inch x 20 inch foam slabs: 2 thick, 1 medium-size, 3 or 4 thin
  - plastic bucket with lid (approximately 8 inches high) • colored chalk
  - large scissors • brown, red, green and yellow latex paint • paintbrush

- **Preparation**
  - Foam slabs of various sizes are available at hardware and fabric stores.
  - You may be able to recycle a foam mattress or some old furniture cushions.
  - If thin foam slabs are unavailable, ask an adult to carefully cut a thicker slab in half with scissors or a serrated bread knife.

- **Instructions**

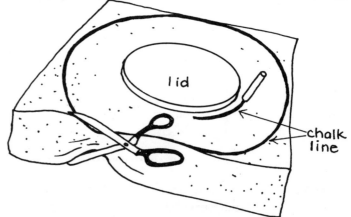

1. The two thick foam slabs will be your hamburger bun. Pile your foam slabs on top of one another, with one thick slab on the bottom. Leave off the other thick slab (the top bun) for now. Your pile should be as high as the plastic bucket; if not, add another slab of foam.

2. With chalk, trace around the bucket lid in the center of every foam slab except for the top bun slab. Cut out the circles. (Save all your leftover foam for other projects.)

3. Draw a large chalk circle on each thick foam slab to form the outside rounded edge of the bun. Do the same for the medium-size slab and one thin slab to form the rounded meat patty and tomato slice.

4. Draw a wavy line around the edge of one thin slab for a lettuce leaf, a square on another for a cheese slice and, if you like, an oval on another thin slab for a pickle slice.

5. Cut out all the shapes. Snip the top of the top bun carefully with scissors to give it a curved, bun shape.

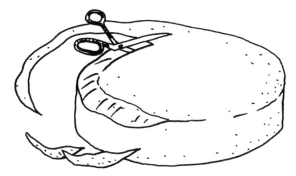

6. Paint the sides and top of each slab in the appropriate color. Mix brown and green for the color of the pickle, and mix brown and yellow for the color of the hamburger bun. When dry, flip the slabs over and paint the other side.

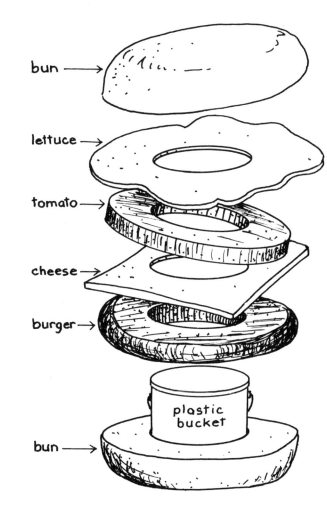

bun →

lettuce →

tomato →

cheese →

burger →

plastic bucket

bun →

7. Stack the foam burger parts around the bucket and place the top bun slab on top.

● **VARIATION**

• Make a hotdog pillow by cutting a piece of foam into a wiener shape and covering it with a nylon stocking knotted at both ends.

• For a hotdog bun, slip a square foam slab into a beige T-shirt. Tuck in the sleeves and ends, and stitch the slab into place around the hotdog. Squeeze on fabric paint to look like ketchup, mustard and relish.

SAUSAGE CHAIR

Stuff some knit tubing to make a chair that squishes to fit around you.

● **MATERIALS**
- 5 feet knit tubing • styrofoam packing pellets or shredded foam

● **PREPARATION**
- You can find a wide variety of knit tubing at a fabric store; it is available in many types, colors and widths. The wider the knit tubing is, the larger your sausage chair will be.

- Ask a furniture or hardware store to save you some styrofoam packing pellets. You can also use lots and lots of popped popcorn made by a hot air popper, without oil or salt. For a softer stuffing, tear up some old foam slabs into tiny pieces.

● **INSTRUCTIONS**
1. Tie an overhand knot at one end of the tubing, as shown. Pull the knot tight so it won't come undone.

2. Through the open end, stuff the tubing with the stuffing you've chosen. Don't pack the stuffing in too tightly or the tube won't be squishy enough.

overhand knot

knit tubing

overhand knot →

3. Twist the open end of the tubing and tie it in a tight overhand knot.

4. Lay your sausage chair on the floor. Sit down at one end of it and wiggle a little until the chair forms around you.

- **VARIATION 1**
  - Make your chair from an old knit dress or a few old sweatshirts sewn together.

- **VARIATION 2**
  - Stuff colorful material tubes or recycled knee-socks or tights to make the letters of your name. Stitch one end of each tube shut with a needle and sturdy thread. (Socks and tights will already be closed at one end.)

  - For letters such as B and A, stuff your tubes with polyester stuffing or soft rags. Sew up the open ends. Bend the tubes into letter shapes and sew them to hold their shape.

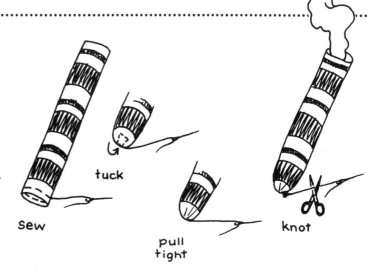

sew   tuck   pull tight   knot

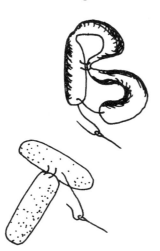

  - For letters such as C and S, cut a cardboard shape of the letter, pull the tubing around it and stuff it on both sides of the cardboard shape. For letters such as T, F and X, make two or three tubes to stuff and sew together.

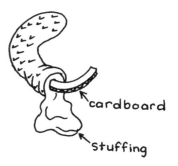

cardboard
stuffing

  - Hang these soft decorations on the wall or prop them up on a shelf.

BOOKSHELVES

Turn some old cardboard boxes into fabulous bookshelves.

- **MATERIALS**
  - cardboard boxes • masking tape, 1½ inches wide • scissors
  - self-adhesive vinyl (from a hardware store) or wallpaper • white glue

- **PREPARATION**
  - Gather some cardboard boxes from around your home, or ask for some at a store. You will need the kind with four flaps at their opening. The sturdiest boxes are those that are square or almost square.

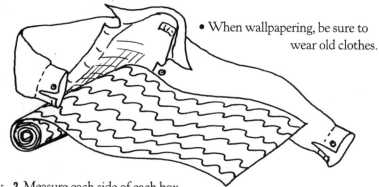

  - When wallpapering, be sure to wear old clothes.

- **INSTRUCTIONS**

  1. Push the flaps of each box firmly to the inside and tape them down securely.

  2. Measure each side of each box, both inside and out. Cut pieces of self-adhesive vinyl or wallpaper about an inch larger than your measurements. Cover each side, using the extra bit of vinyl to wrap around the box edges.

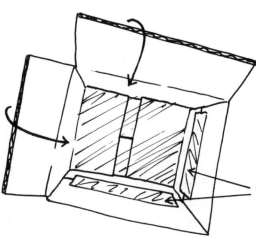

tape

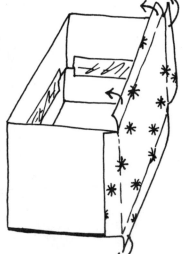

3. Arrange the boxes against a wall in a corner with the largest ones on the bottom. Stack the boxes no more than three high. Glue them together to make your shelves sturdier.

4. Store your heaviest books and objects on the lower shelves. The upper shelves are better for storing light items.

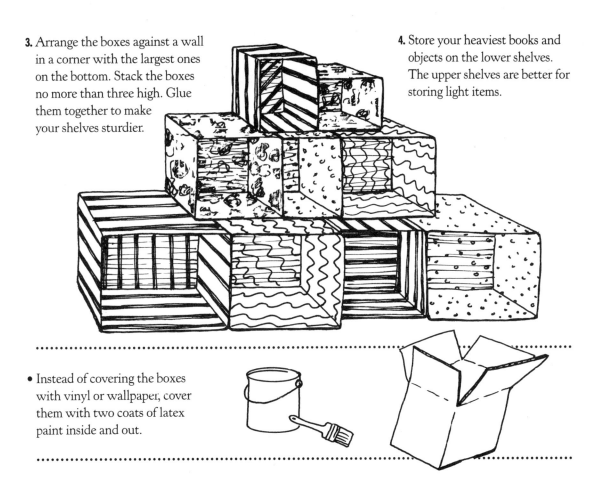

● **VARIATION 1**

- Instead of covering the boxes with vinyl or wallpaper, cover them with two coats of latex paint inside and out.

● **VARIATION 2**

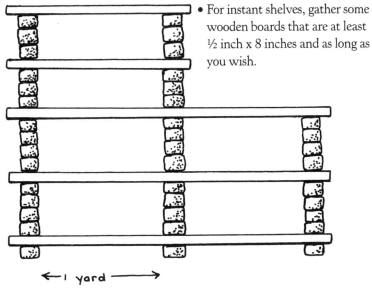

← 1 yard →

- For instant shelves, gather some wooden boards that are at least ½ inch x 8 inches and as long as you wish.

- Against a wall, stack the boards one at a time on top of bricks or sturdy blocks placed no more than 1 yard apart.

- The bricks and blocks should be stacked no more than 1 yard high, with the widest and longest boards on the bottom and the smallest on top.

BRAIDED RUG

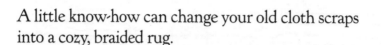

A little know-how can change your old cloth scraps into a cozy, braided rug.

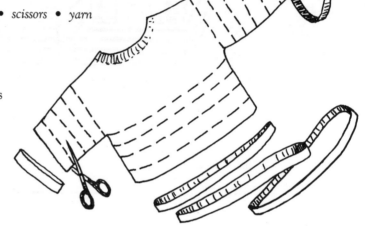

- **MATERIALS**
  - old T-shirts, sweatshirts or socks • scissors • yarn
  - 2 twist ties • darning needle

- **PREPARATION**
  - Collect several old T-shirts, socks or sweatshirts from around the house. Cut across the garments to make loops of fabric 1 inch to 2 inches wide. (Always get permission before cutting up old clothing.)

- **INSTRUCTIONS**

1. Tie three T-shirt loops together at one end with a piece of yarn. Use a twist tie to fasten this end to the back of a chair.

2. Fold the right loop over between the other two loops. Then fold the left loop over between the other two loops.

3. Keep folding, or braiding, the loops tightly together. When a loop gets short, attach a new loop to the end with a loop knot as shown.

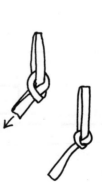

4. When your braid reaches several yards in length, use a twist tie to hold the ends in place.

5. Twist the beginning of the braid into a spiral shape for a round rug, or an oval shape for an oval rug. Double a length of yarn on a darning needle and sew the braid together. Push the needle between the braided loops of the rug and pull each stitch tight to hold the rug together.

round rug

oval rug

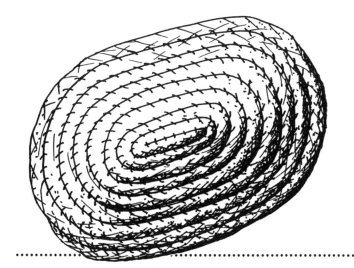

6. Lay the rug on a flat surface and continue arranging the braid and sewing. When you've sewn to the end of the braid, undo the twist tie, add more loops and continue braiding.

7. When your rug reaches the size you want, braid until the loop ends are very short and stitch them to the rug.

● **VARIATION**

• Add a fringe to your rug. Cut several pieces of yarn the same length.

• Fold a piece of yarn in half. Poke a crochet hook down through a hole along the edge of your rug.

• Place the piece of folded yarn in the hook and pull the crochet hook back up through the hole.

• Remove the hook, push the ends of the yarn around and through the loop as shown, then pull them tight. Repeat around the entire edge of the rug.

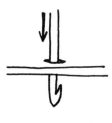
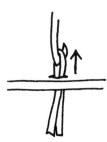
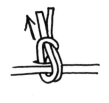

LAMPSHADE

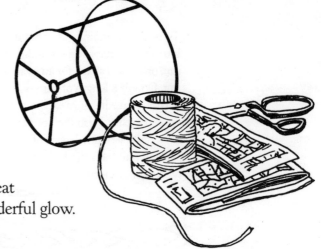

From a basic wire frame, make a great woven lampshade that casts a wonderful glow.

- **MATERIALS**
  - wire lampshade form (at least 1 foot wide) • paint (optional) • heavy string • masking tape
  - weaving material (fabric, wrapping paper or old road maps) • white glue • lamp • 40-watt lightbulb

- **PREPARATION**
  - Take the covering off an old lampshade or buy a wire form at a craft store. If you like, paint the wire to suit the color of your weaving material.

  - Your lampshade form needs an uneven number of struts 1 inch to 2 inches apart. To add one or more struts, tie string with a loop knot to the top ring of the form, stretch it taut, and tie it tightly to the bottom ring. Tape the loose ends as shown.

1-2 inches

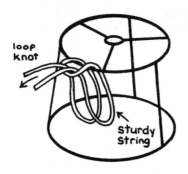

loop knot

sturdy string

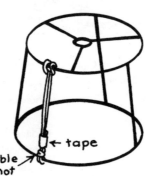

← tape

double knot

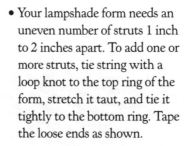

fabric

  - Prepare your weaving material. If you are using fabric, rip it into long strips 1 inch to 2 inches wide. Or cut paper into strips; wet and twist them into rope-like strands.

wet paper

- **INSTRUCTIONS**

1. Wrap the end of a piece of weaving material around the bottom of a strut. Weave in and out of the struts, pulling your material snug and pushing it down as you go.

2. Start weaving with a new piece of material where the first piece ends. Overlap the two ends. Continue until the form is covered.

3. Tuck any loose ends into the weaving so they don't show, and use glue to hold them in place.

overlapping section

4. Fasten the lampshade to your lamp and screw in the lightbulb. Make sure that the woven lampshade is at least 4 inches away from the lightbulb.

- **VARIATION**

- Design a starry lampshade for your wire form. Draw a pattern for your lampshade on a wide strip of paper, and add tabs around the top and bottom for gluing onto the form. Trace your pattern onto a road map or a large sheet of heavy paper and cut it out.

- Place the paper on a thick towel with the good side up, and punch holes in linear, circular or spiral patterns with a small nail or thumbtack. If using a road map, punch small holes along roads and larger holes at cities.

- Wrap the paper around the wire form. Glue the seam and tabs carefully, and attach the lampshade to your lamp.

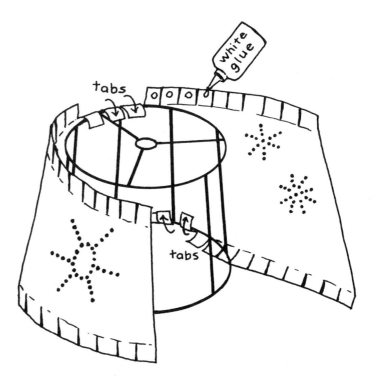

tabs

tabs

white glue

COMFY BED BOLSTER

Snuggle into a comfy, homemade bed bolster while you read or just daydream.

- **MATERIALS**
  - large, old sweatshirt or sweater • darning needle • yarn
  - soft rags, shredded foam or polyester stuffing • decorations (fabric paint, sequins, fabric scraps)

stuffing

- **INSTRUCTIONS**

  1. Turn the sweatshirt or sweater so that its softest surface is facing out.

  2. Thread a darning needle with a double length of yarn and knot the end. Use an overhand stitch to sew the neck of the sweatshirt shut, pulling tight as you sew. Secure it with a good knot.

  3. Tuck the ends of the sleeves in, leaving about 10 inches of each sleeve hanging out. Sew the sleeves closed.

  4. Stuff the sleeves and body of the sweatshirt with your chosen stuffing. Then sew the waist-band tightly shut.

  5. Decorate your homemade bed bolster.

- **VARIATION 1**

- Stuff the body of an old, white T-shirt to make a soft-sculpture face pillow. Pull the sleeves, the open waist and the neck around to the back of the T-shirt.

- Slip a piece of flesh-colored panty hose over the T-shirt and knot the ends to hold everything in place.

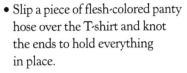

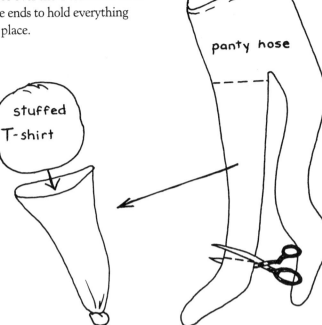

- Use a needle with flesh-colored thread to stitch from back to front and back again to form facial features. Pull these stitches tight to form indentations for the features.

- Add some powdered blush on the cheeks and sew on yarn for hair. Sew on buttons for eyes if you want them to appear open.

- **VARIATION 2**

- Make a soft-sculpture person pillow. Stuff two pairs of old tights for arms and legs. Sew one pair shut for arms and place them inside a T-shirt, with one stuffed arm hanging out of each sleeve. Stitch them into place.

- Make a stuffed head, as in Variation 1, and sew it tightly onto the neck of the T-shirt. Stuff the T-shirt to form the body. Sew the open waist of the stuffed legs to the bottom of the T-shirt body.

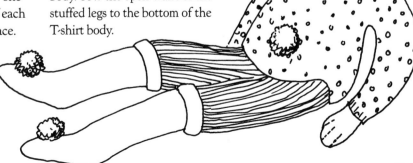

HEADBOARD COVER

Paint cardboard with vivid squiggles, spirals and swirls to create a modern folk-art headboard.

● **MATERIALS**
- *2 large pieces of corrugated cardboard* • *chalk* • *scissors* • *white glue* • *heavy objects*
- *masking tape* • *assorted colors of latex paint* • *paintbrushes* • *small, plastic squeeze bottles*

● **PREPARATION**
- Find two pieces of cardboard that are larger than your bed's current headboard. A discarded packing case is a good source.
- Wear old clothes and cover your work surface with newspapers.

● **INSTRUCTIONS**

1. Using chalk, draw the outline of your headboard on a piece of cardboard. Then draw as large a shape as possible around your headboard outline.

2. Cut out the larger shape. Trace it onto the second piece of cardboard and cut this out as well.

chalk

chalk

3. Use lots of glue to attach the two large cardboard shapes at the edges; only the bottom edge should be left open. Place some heavy objects on top to hold things in place until the glue is dry. Then cover any rough edges with masking tape.

4. Plan your headboard design in chalk. Paint the front and back with two coats of latex paint, letting it dry between coats.

5. Squeeze paint from small, plastic squeeze bottles to make squiggles, spirals and other fun details.

6. Let your new headboard cover dry and slip it over your headboard.

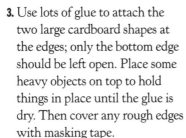

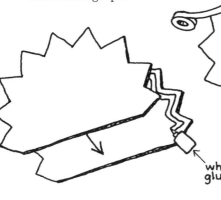

white glue

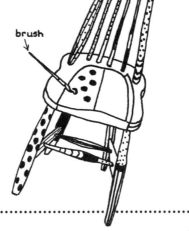

- • **VARIATION 1**

- Find an old chair and, with permission, paint it to match your modern folk-art headboard.

brush

- Use a large brush to paint on the base color. With a smaller brush or squeeze bottle, add details.

- • **VARIATION 2**

- Instead of painting your cardboard headboard, cover it with a collage of favorite comics or pictures.

- Mix equal parts of white glue and water. Dip cut-out comics or pictures in the glue mixture and stick them onto the headboard cover. Overlap the edges if you like.

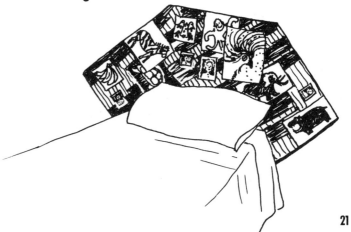

ORGANIZERS: INTRODUCTION

- Keeping your room in order can be a chore. When all your stuff is jumbled together, it can look like a mess (especially to your parents), but if you organize a few places to store or display your belongings, your room will look terrific as well as tidy.

- Collect paper tubes, cardboard, news-papers, paint, white glue, scissors, odd socks, stones and string from around the house and garden. Now you're ready to get organized!

- If you have lots of pencils, papers and books, keep them together with a personalized pencil holder, a handy bulletin board and some friendly bookends. Feed your garbage to a big-mouthed garbage gobbler made of papier-mâché.

• Your stuffed animals will be happy to sleep together in a handy hammock. And your card collection will be safe in a treasure box. Are your clothes spread all over your room? Make a clothes rack or hanger for the clean stuff and a hungry laundry gobbler for the dirty stuff.

• Several medium-size screws hold up a bulletin board, clothes rack or clothes hoop. Ask an adult to help you. Use a stud finder from the hardware store to find the solid parts of your wall. Or use plastic screw anchors, which fit into drilled holes in plaster walls to hold the screws firmly in place.

So you think tossing your laundry in a washing machine is a tough chore? One hundred years ago, you might have found yourself bent over a washboard. After scrubbing and rinsing clothes with handpumped water and hanging them to dry, you'd have to remove all of the wrinkles with an iron that had to be reheated every ten minutes on top of a woodstove. The woodstove, of course, would be fuelled with firewood that you had to chop. Now *that's* hard work!

Yurt, laavu, tipi: these are all names for nomad homes. Nomads keep very few possessions; in fact, they can pack everything they own and carry it away at a moment's notice. Once they reach their destination, they can put up their homes and have all of their possessions in place in less than two hours. Whew!

BULLETIN BOARD

Organize all those reminders, notes
and lists on an easy-to-make bulletin board.

- **MATERIALS**
  - *2 large pieces of corrugated cardboard* • *pencil* • *sturdy scissors* • *white glue*
  - *latex paint and paintbrushes, or large piece of felt* • *several nails*

- **PREPARATION**
  - Decide where you want to hang your bulletin board and how large you want it to be.
  - Check appliance or furniture stores for a large cardboard box. Cut two large pieces of corrugated cardboard to the size you need.
  - If you can't find large enough pieces, tape smaller pieces of cardboard together with masking tape.

- **INSTRUCTIONS**
  1. Design a simple shape for your bulletin board such as a circle, star, animal or flower.

  2. Draw your design on one piece of cardboard and cut it out. Trace the cardboard shape onto the other piece of cardboard and cut it out.

cardboard

  3. Use a scrap of cardboard to spread a thin layer of white glue over one cardboard shape. Place the second shape on top of the first, lining up the edges. Press to make sure the two pieces are well glued.

4. Paint the top and sides of the cardboard bulletin board. Or glue on a large piece of felt cut in the same shape.

5. Ask an adult to help you hang your bulletin board. A nail hammered in at each corner should hold it up.

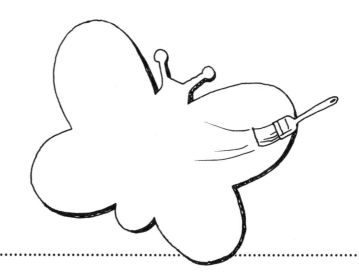

● **VARIATION 1**

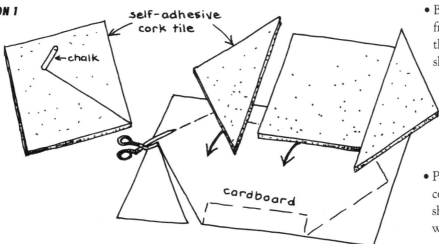

self-adhesive cork tile

←chalk

cardboard

• Buy some self-adhesive cork tiles from a hardware store and cut them into shapes. Cut matching shapes from heavy cardboard.

• Peel off the backing and stick the cork shapes onto the cardboard shapes. Fasten each to the wall with two nails.

● **VARIATION 2**

• For a large bulletin board, buy a white sheet of soft particleboard, called prime-coated tentest, from a lumber yard. Cover the rough edges with plastic, snap-on shelf edging (also from a lumber yard), which can be cut to size with scissors. Use strong nails or screws to hang it.

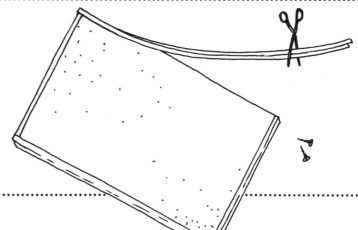

● **VARIATION 3**

• Hang a small quilt or felt banner for use as a bulletin board. Use safety pins to attach your notes and lists.

BOOKENDS

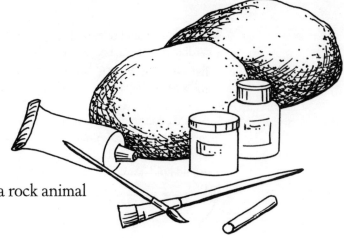

Go on a rock hunt. Then paint a rock animal
or two to hold up your books.

● **MATERIALS**
- smooth rocks • acrylic or latex paint • paintbrush • water • jar lid
- chalk • felt piece (optional) • pompon (optional)

● **PREPARATION**

- Find some smooth, rounded rocks that are 4 inches to 8 inches wide. Wash off any dirt and dry them.

- Choose one rock from your collection and study it. Decide what animal it looks like and which lump or indentation suggests an eye, ear, nose or tail.

- Cover your work surface with newspaper.

● **INSTRUCTIONS**

1. Choose one main color to paint your rock animal. For instance, use green for a frog, white for a rabbit, pink for a pig, orange for a cat and brown for a porcupine or a beaver.

2. Paint the entire surface of your rock with the color you've chosen.

jar lid

acrylic paint

3. Set the painted rock in an upside-down jar lid to dry. When dry, paint a second coat if necessary.

4. After the rock has dried, use chalk to sketch on the animal's legs, ears and other features.

chalk →

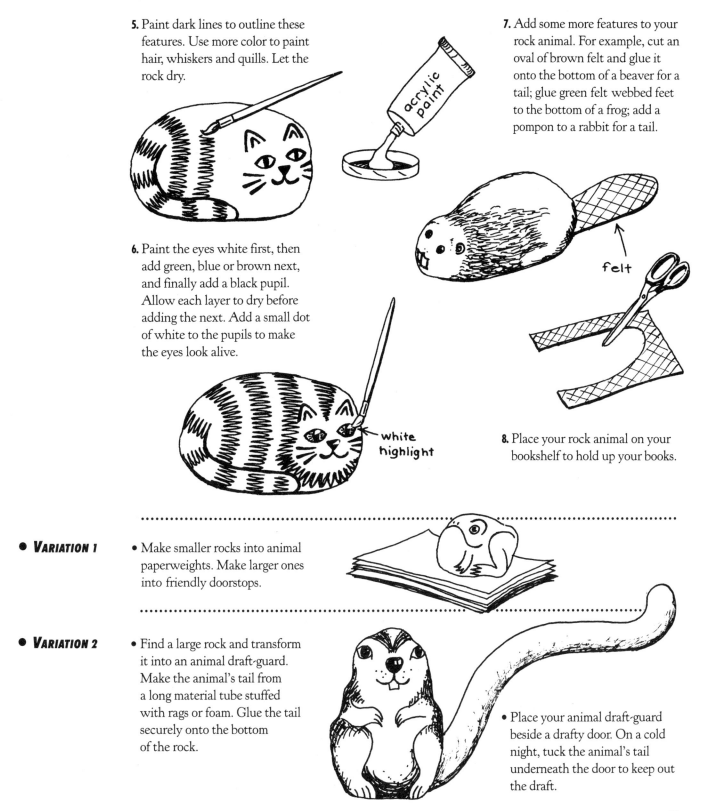

5. Paint dark lines to outline these features. Use more color to paint hair, whiskers and quills. Let the rock dry.

6. Paint the eyes white first, then add green, blue or brown next, and finally add a black pupil. Allow each layer to dry before adding the next. Add a small dot of white to the pupils to make the eyes look alive.

white highlight

acrylic paint

7. Add some more features to your rock animal. For example, cut an oval of brown felt and glue it onto the bottom of a beaver for a tail; glue green felt webbed feet to the bottom of a frog; add a pompon to a rabbit for a tail.

felt

8. Place your rock animal on your bookshelf to hold up your books.

● **VARIATION 1**
- Make smaller rocks into animal paperweights. Make larger ones into friendly doorstops.

● **VARIATION 2**
- Find a large rock and transform it into an animal draft-guard. Make the animal's tail from a long material tube stuffed with rags or foam. Glue the tail securely onto the bottom of the rock.

- Place your animal draft-guard beside a drafty door. On a cold night, tuck the animal's tail underneath the door to keep out the draft.

PENCIL ORGANIZER

Make a paper-tube pencil holder to keep your pencils, pens, erasers and rulers in one place.

● **MATERIALS**
● assorted paper tubes ● scissors ● decorations (self-adhesive vinyl, comics, wrapping paper, confetti, stickers, paint) ● large piece of cardboard ● white glue

● **INSTRUCTIONS**

1. Cut paper tubes to different lengths. For variety, cut some on an angle.

2. Decorate each paper tube with comics, paint, colorful paper, confetti, stickers or self-adhesive vinyl. Use one method or combine several.

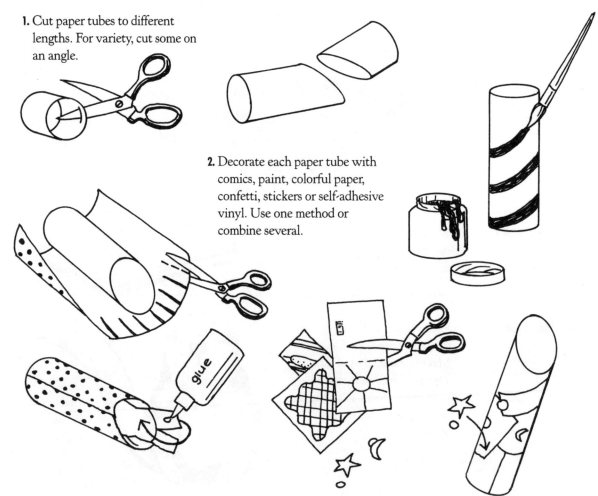

3. Fasten the paper tubes to a cardboard base. Begin with your tallest tube. Glue it securely to the base using lots of glue.

4. Place a second tube next to the first, gluing it to the cardboard base as well as to the first tube. Add more tubes, gluing each one to the others as well as to the cardboard base.

5. Let the glue dry. Cut off the excess cardboard from around the tubes.

● **VARIATION**

- Make a paper-tube wall shelf to store and display all your tiny knickknacks.

- Cut paper tubes to lengths of exactly 1 inch. Glue the tubes close together onto a piece of cardboard. Let the glue dry.

- Trim off the excess cardboard. Leave some cardboard around the outside of the tubes so you can hang your shelf on the wall. Paint it, hang it, and tuck in all your tiny treasures.

29

ANIMAL HAMMOCK

Knot together a cozy, corner
hammock to hold all your stuffed animals.

- **MATERIALS**
  - 35 yards heavy string, cord or twine • scissors • 3 metal rings or large washers (from a hardware store)
  - masking tape • 3 small hooks (from a hardware store)

- **PREPARATION**
  - Cut one piece of string 4 feet long. Cut 12 more pieces, each 8 feet long.

- **INSTRUCTIONS**

1. Tie a metal ring securely to each end of the 4-foot piece of string. Fasten each ring to something solid so that the string is pulled tight horizontally.

2. Fold each of the 12 remaining strings in half and attach them, one at a time, to the horizontal string with a loop knot as shown. Space them about 3 inches apart.

3. Starting at one end, slip the outside string through the metal ring. Tie the next two strings together in an overhand knot about 3 inches below the horizontal string. Continue tying each pair of strings until you reach the last string. Tuck it through the metal ring at that end.

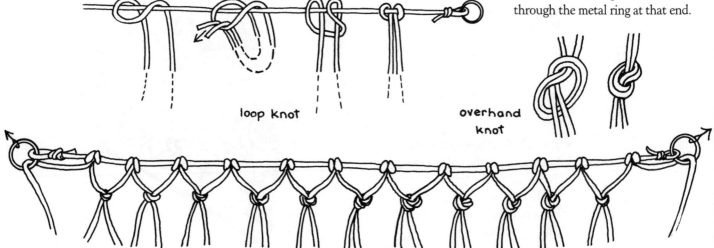

loop knot

overhand knot

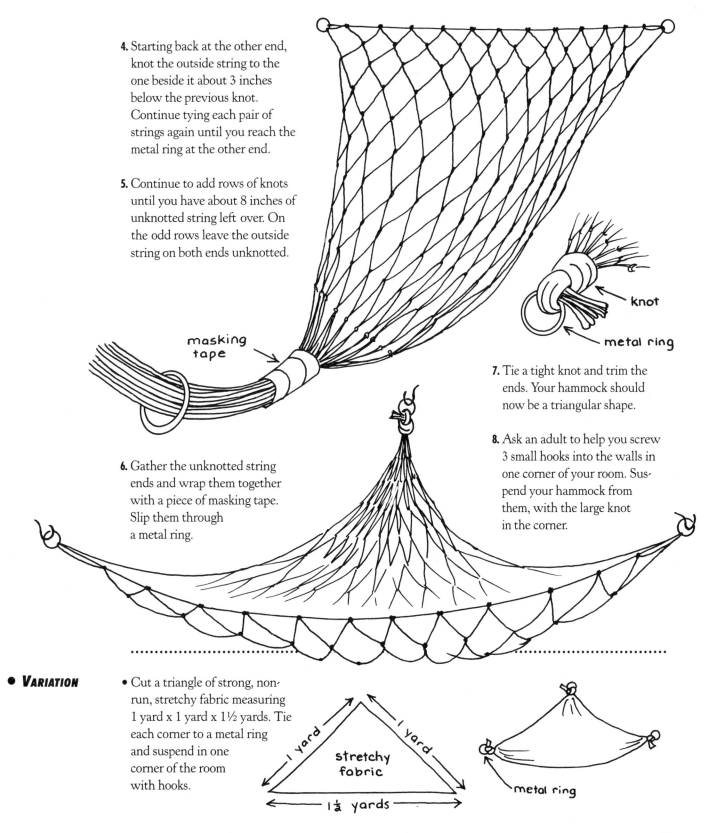

4. Starting back at the other end, knot the outside string to the one beside it about 3 inches below the previous knot. Continue tying each pair of strings again until you reach the metal ring at the other end.

5. Continue to add rows of knots until you have about 8 inches of unknotted string left over. On the odd rows leave the outside string on both ends unknotted.

masking tape

knot

metal ring

7. Tie a tight knot and trim the ends. Your hammock should now be a triangular shape.

8. Ask an adult to help you screw 3 small hooks into the walls in one corner of your room. Suspend your hammock from them, with the large knot in the corner.

6. Gather the unknotted string ends and wrap them together with a piece of masking tape. Slip them through a metal ring.

● **VARIATION**

● Cut a triangle of strong, non-run, stretchy fabric measuring 1 yard x 1 yard x 1½ yards. Tie each corner to a metal ring and suspend in one corner of the room with hooks.

1 yard

1 yard

stretchy fabric

1½ yards

metal ring

31

GARBAGE GOBBLER

With a little imagination, create
a papier-mâché monster that loves to gobble garbage.

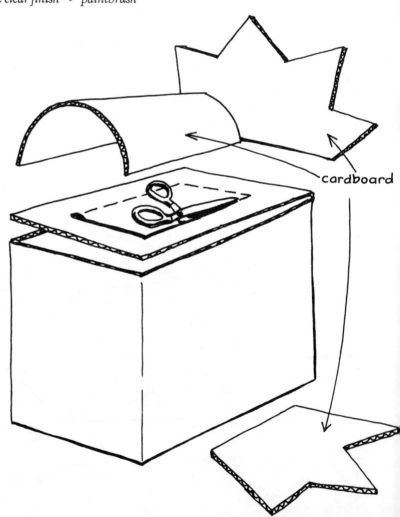

cardboard

- **MATERIALS**
  - sturdy cardboard box • 3 cups water • 2 cups flour • ⅔ cup salt • large bowl • scissors
  - large paper or plastic cylinder (or piece of cardboard) • masking tape • extra cardboard • newspaper
  - latex paint, or tempera paint and a clear finish • paintbrush

- **PREPARATION**
  - Find a cardboard box that has one large flap as a lid or a separate lid that fits over the top. A grocery store probably has one.

  - Combine the water, flour and salt in a large bowl. This is your papier-mâché paste. Mix more as you need it.

  - Tear some newspaper into thin strips for your papier-mâché modelling.

- **INSTRUCTIONS**
  1. Cut a large opening in the lid of the cardboard box.

  2. Cut the cylinder lengthwise and, with masking tape, fasten it to the lid over the hole. If you don't have a cylinder, bend a piece of cardboard into a half-cylinder shape and tape it on. This will be your garbage gobbler's mouth.

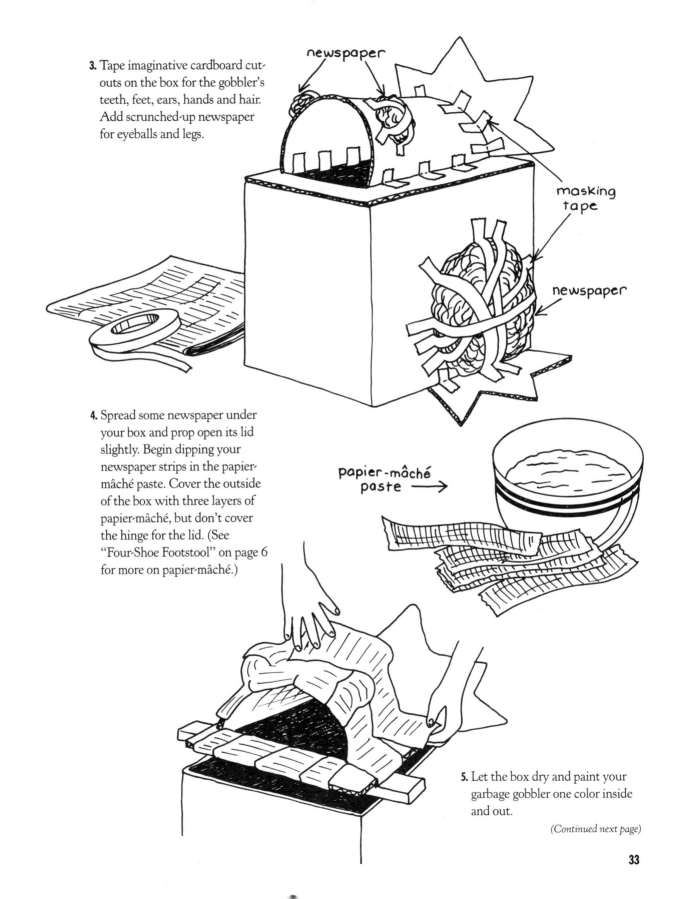

3. Tape imaginative cardboard cut-outs on the box for the gobbler's teeth, feet, ears, hands and hair. Add scrunched-up newspaper for eyeballs and legs.

newspaper

masking tape

newspaper

4. Spread some newspaper under your box and prop open its lid slightly. Begin dipping your newspaper strips in the papier-mâché paste. Cover the outside of the box with three layers of papier-mâché, but don't cover the hinge for the lid. (See "Four-Shoe Footstool" on page 6 for more on papier-mâché.)

papier-mâché paste →

5. Let the box dry and paint your garbage gobbler one color inside and out.

(Continued next page)

6. After the first coat is dry, add details in striking colors to create lots of character for your creature. You might want to give it polka dots, stripes, scales, warts or fur.

7. If you have used tempera paint, brush a clear finish onto your completed garbage gobbler.

• **VARIATION**

• Find a tall, sturdy cardboard box with a large, hinged flap for a lid. On one side of the box near the top, draw a rectangle and cut along the two sides and the bottom. Fold the flap back and forth until it swings freely.

• Cover the box with a collage of comics, wrapping paper or self-adhesive vinyl. Or decorate it with paints, markers or stickers.

• Take aim at the hole with your garbage. Just lift the large, hinged flap to empty the box when it gets full.

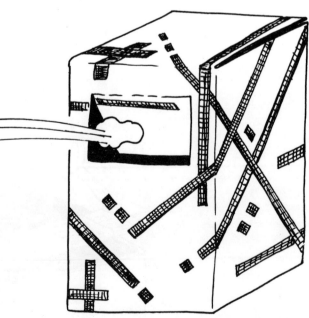

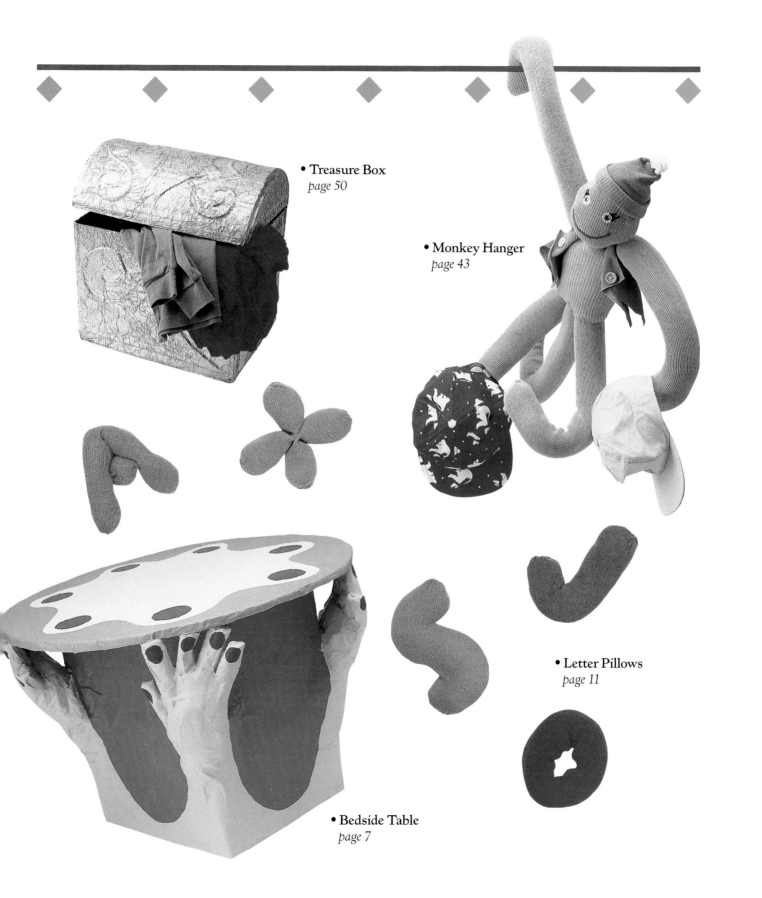

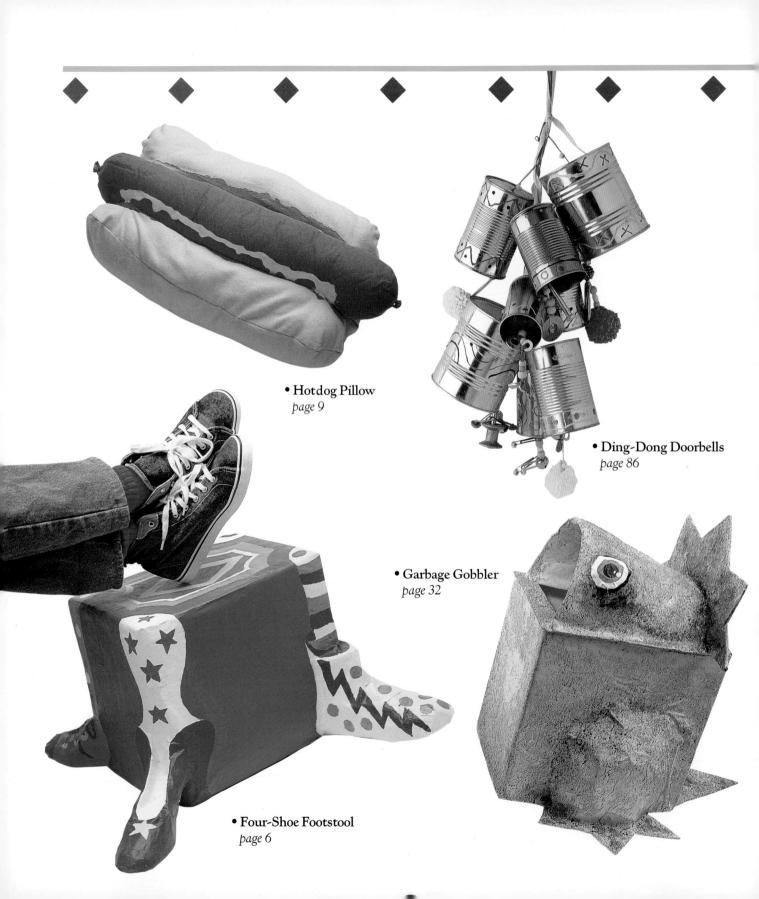

• Hotdog Pillow
page 9

• Ding-Dong Doorbells
page 86

• Garbage Gobbler
page 32

• Four-Shoe Footstool
page 6

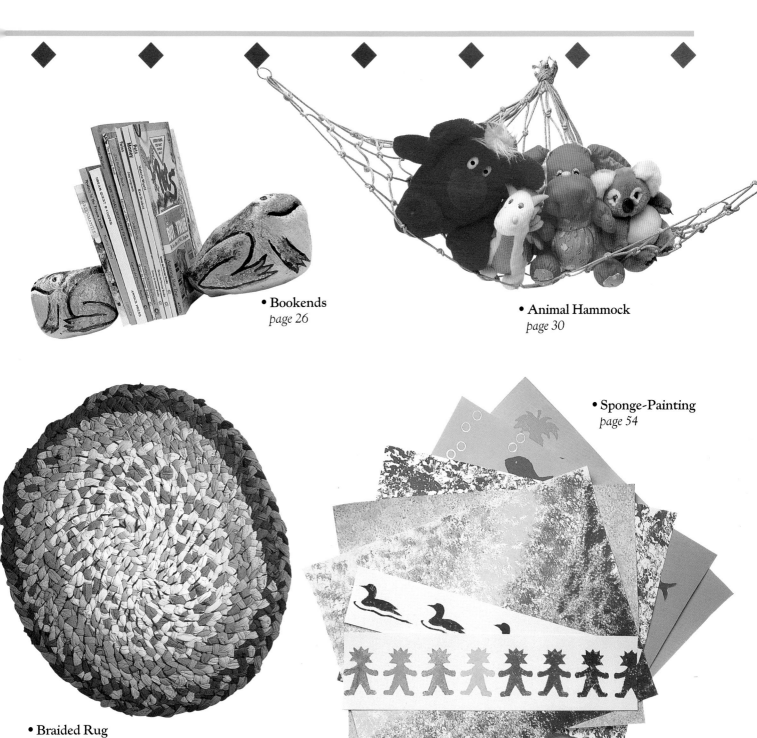

• Bookends
page 26

• Animal Hammock
page 30

• Sponge-Painting
page 54

• Braided Rug
page 14

• Stencilled Border
page 56

• Laundry Gobbler
page 48

• Fabric Family Collage
page 76

• Bookshelves
page 12

• Pillow Person
page 19

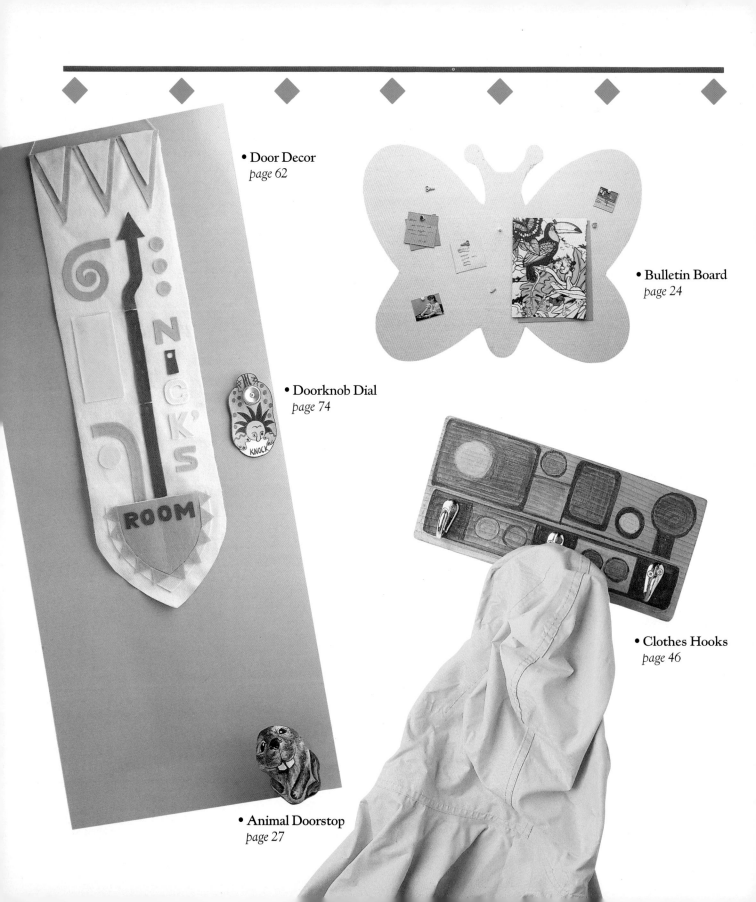

• Door Decor
page 62

• Bulletin Board
page 24

• Doorknob Dial
page 74

• Clothes Hooks
page 46

• Animal Doorstop
page 27

MONKEY HANGER

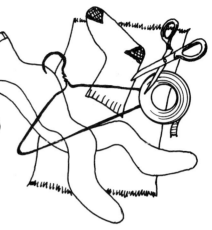

Make a monkey hanger that will happily hold your stuff with its arms, legs and tail.

● **MATERIALS**
  - 3 wire coat hangers • soft rags or soft, old clothing • masking tape • newspaper
  - 4 stocking legs from tights or panty hose • fabric paint • needle and thread • brightly colored odd sock

● **PREPARATION**
  - Cut several rags or pieces of soft, old clothing into strips 4 to 6 inches wide.

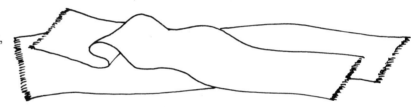

● **INSTRUCTIONS**

1. Unbend three wire hangers, and form a loop on the end of one.

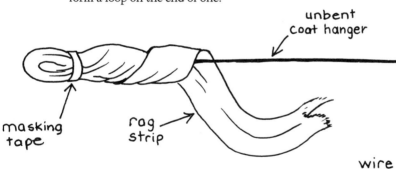

masking tape

rag strip

unbent coat hanger

2. Wrap the two straight wires with cloth strips. Use masking tape to hold the ends in place. Each wrapped straight wire should measure about the width of your wrist. These will become the arms and legs on your monkey hanger.

3. Scrunch some newspaper into a ball and push it in the loop of the third wire. Use masking tape to hold it in place. This will become the head on your monkey hanger.

wire →

crumpled newspaper

masking tape

(Continued next page)

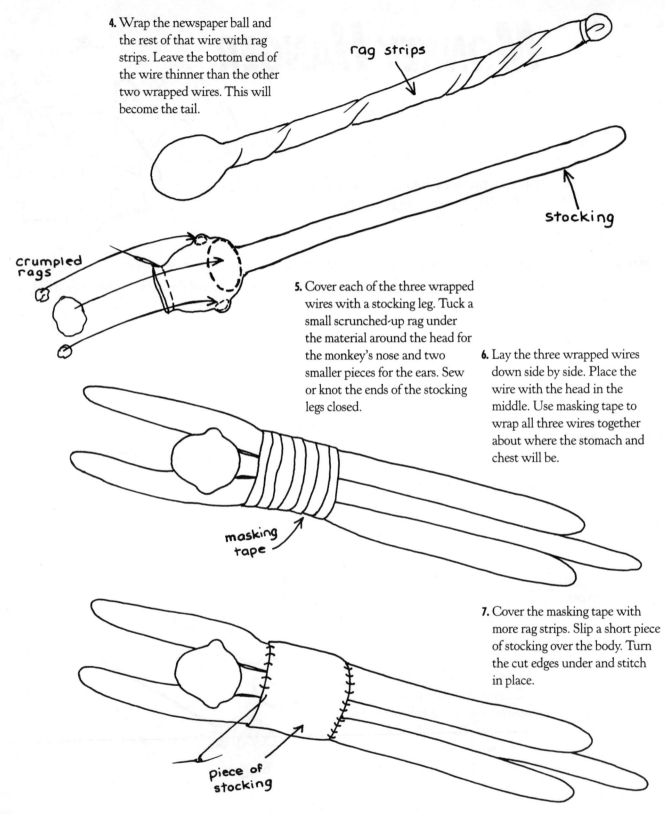

4. Wrap the newspaper ball and the rest of that wire with rag strips. Leave the bottom end of the wire thinner than the other two wrapped wires. This will become the tail.

rag strips

stocking

crumpled rags

5. Cover each of the three wrapped wires with a stocking leg. Tuck a small scrunched-up rag under the material around the head for the monkey's nose and two smaller pieces for the ears. Sew or knot the ends of the stocking legs closed.

6. Lay the three wrapped wires down side by side. Place the wire with the head in the middle. Use masking tape to wrap all three wires together about where the stomach and chest will be.

masking tape

7. Cover the masking tape with more rag strips. Slip a short piece of stocking over the body. Turn the cut edges under and stitch in place.

piece of stocking

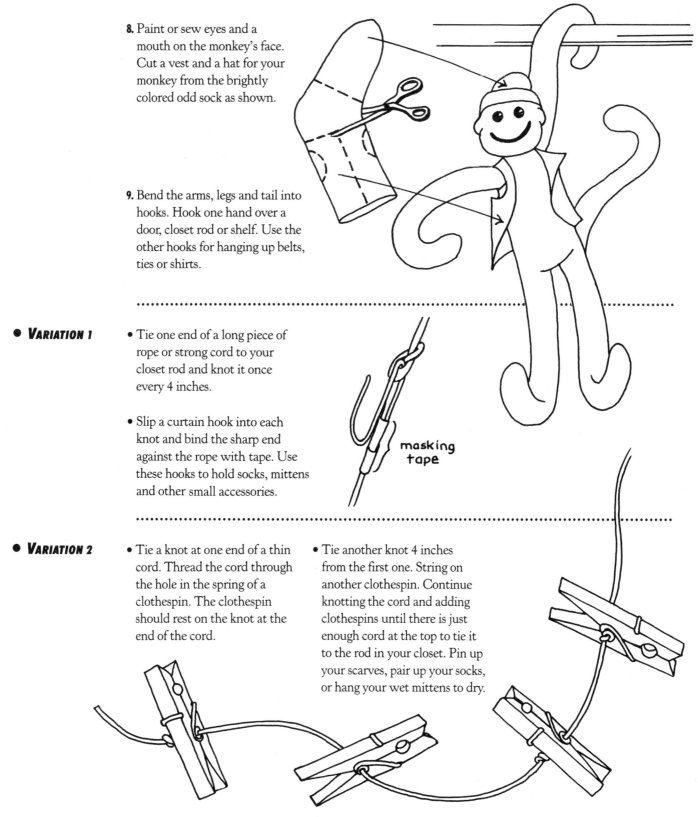

8. Paint or sew eyes and a mouth on the monkey's face. Cut a vest and a hat for your monkey from the brightly colored odd sock as shown.

9. Bend the arms, legs and tail into hooks. Hook one hand over a door, closet rod or shelf. Use the other hooks for hanging up belts, ties or shirts.

● **VARIATION 1**

• Tie one end of a long piece of rope or strong cord to your closet rod and knot it once every 4 inches.

• Slip a curtain hook into each knot and bind the sharp end against the rope with tape. Use these hooks to hold socks, mittens and other small accessories.

masking tape

● **VARIATION 2**

• Tie a knot at one end of a thin cord. Thread the cord through the hole in the spring of a clothespin. The clothespin should rest on the knot at the end of the cord.

• Tie another knot 4 inches from the first one. String on another clothespin. Continue knotting the cord and adding clothespins until there is just enough cord at the top to tie it to the rod in your closet. Pin up your scarves, pair up your socks, or hang your wet mittens to dry.

CLOTHES RACK

Don't throw your clothes over a chair! Make a customized clothes rack and hang them up.

- **MATERIALS**
  - 1 inch x 8 inch x 12 inch cedar board (from a lumber yard) • paper and pencil • sandpaper
  - hammer • assorted screwdrivers and nails • wood finish • 2 coat hooks • 2 large nails or screws

- **PREPARATION**
  - Find a place where you can hammer without bothering anyone; try the basement or outdoors on the grass, on a patio, on a balcony or on your doorstep.

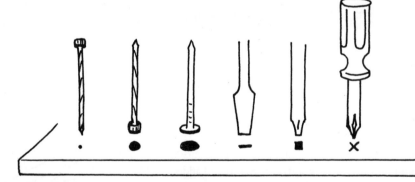

  - Practise hammering designs on a small scrap of soft wood or on the back of your cedar board. Use different screwdrivers and nails for different shapes as shown.

  - On paper, trace the outline of your cedar board and plan your design.

- **INSTRUCTIONS**
  1. Sand the edges of the cedar board so they are smooth and rounded.

  2. Place your paper design on top of the board and trace the outlines of your sections with a pencil, pushing down hard. The pencil will dent the soft wood underneath.

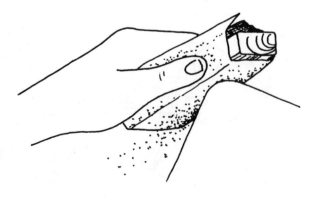

3. With a hammer and a flat screwdriver, tap in the pencil indentations of the outlines first. Then tap different objects to make different designs on the board. Make circles with the round head of a nail, stars with an X-tipped screwdriver, and small dots with a nail tip. Fill in the background by tapping nail-head circles very close together.

4. After making your design on the board, ask an adult to help you apply a wood finish. It can be furniture wax, wood oil, stain or varnish.

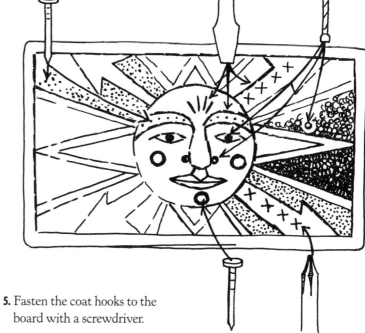

5. Fasten the coat hooks to the board with a screwdriver.

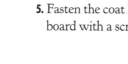

6. Ask an adult to help you hang your clothes rack on a wall or door with two large nails or screws.

• **VARIATION**

• Use water-based markers and pencil crayons to decorate a wooden board. This will give a soft, antique look to the wood. Finish the board with wood oil or wax, add clothes hooks, and mount it on the wall.

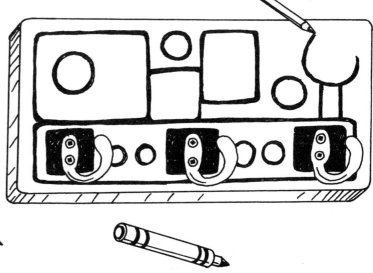

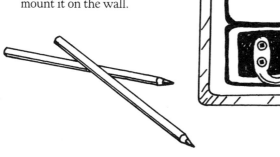

LAUNDRY GOBBLER

Are your dirty clothes everywhere? A hungry laundry gobbler will solve your problem.

● **MATERIALS**
   • pillowcase • newspaper • pencil • scissors • squeeze-on fabric paint, or latex paint and paintbrush • coat hanger • large safety pin • 5 feet sturdy cord

● **PREPARATION**
   • Find an old pillowcase and get permission to use it. Place several sheets of newspaper flat inside it.

● **INSTRUCTIONS**
   1. Draw an 8-inch wide circle on one side of the pillowcase near the closed end. This will become your laundry gobbler's mouth. Cut the circle out of one layer of the pillowcase fabric.

   2. Paint lips around the edges of the mouth to prevent the edges from unravelling. Also paint on eyes, hair and other features. Let the pillowcase dry.

3. Snip a small hole in the closed end of the pillowcase as shown. Slip the coat hanger hook through this hole.

4. Snip a small hole in the hem of the pillowcase. Pin a large safety pin to one end of a piece of cord and thread it through the hole, around the inside of the hem, and out the hole again.

5. Remove the safety pin and knot each end of the cord. Pull on the cord ends and tie them in a large bow.

6. Hang your laundry gobbler from a doorknob, closet rod or hook.

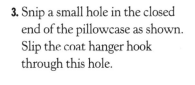

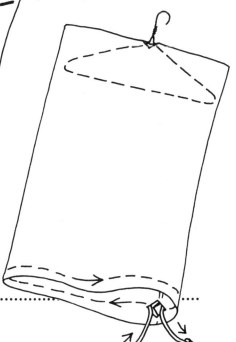

hole

7. When the gobbler is full of laundry, untie the cord, pull open the bottom, and empty it into a laundry basket. Tie the cord up again and hang your gobbler up for another meal.

● **VARIATION**

• If you have an open laundry hamper in your room, make a laundry-ball net for it. Ask an adult to screw a 12-inch wooden embroidery hoop (from a craft store) in the wall just above your laundry hamper.

• Cut ten pieces of string, each 1 yard long. Fold each string in half and tie them with a loop knot around the rim of the embroidery hoop.

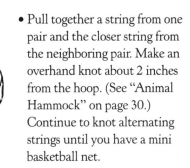

loop knot

• Pull together a string from one pair and the closer string from the neighboring pair. Make an overhand knot about 2 inches from the hoop. (See "Animal Hammock" on page 30.) Continue to knot alternating strings until you have a mini basketball net.

• Place your open laundry hamper under the hoop and score points every time your laundry falls into the hamper.

TREASURE BOX

Stash away your card collections or your favorite mementos in this treasure chest.

- **MATERIALS**
  - *large or small cardboard box with lid* • *scissors* • *extra cardboard* • *masking tape* • *white glue* • *string* • *paintbrush* • *aluminum foil* • *black tempera paint* • *rags or paper towels* • *paper or fabric*

- **PREPARATION**
  - Gather up some used, clean aluminum foil. Or gently crinkle several pieces of new foil and spread them out flat again.

- **INSTRUCTIONS**
  1. Cut out two cardboard half-circles. Tape one on each end of your box lid as shown.

  2. Cut a piece of cardboard as wide as the box lid and bend it around the half-circles, taping as you go. Trim off any excess cardboard.

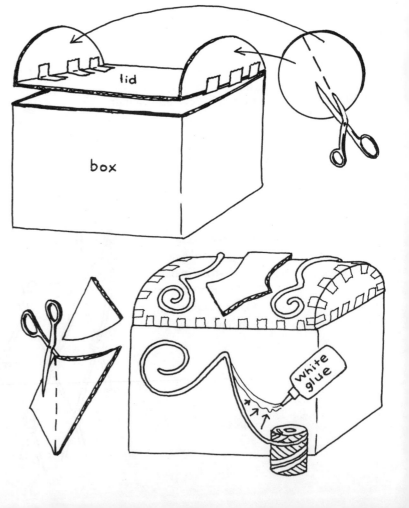

  3. Glue cardboard shapes and string patterns onto the lid and sides of the box. These will form a raised pattern in the foil. Let the box dry.

4. Brush white glue evenly on one side of the box, getting into all the corners, and cover the side with foil. Press the foil down gently so it takes the form of the shapes underneath.

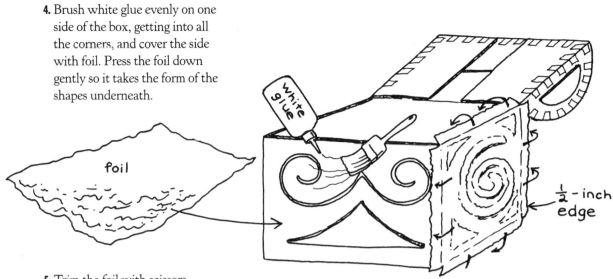

5. Trim the foil with scissors, leaving ½ inch extra on each side. Fold the extra foil around the edges of the box and glue it in place. Repeat this until the entire box is covered. Let the box dry.

6. Paint the foil with black paint. Be sure to get paint into all the little cracks and creases.

7. While the paint is still wet, wipe off as much of it as you can with rags or paper towels. The paint will remain in the crinkles and creases, giving your box an antique appearance.

8. When the box is dry, wipe it with a damp rag. Glue paper or fabric on the inside as a lining.

● **VARIATION**

• Add a false bottom to your box for hiding secret treasures. In the bottom of the box along three sides, glue several layers of ½-inch cardboard strips.

• Cut out a sturdy, cardboard false bottom using the inside measurements of the box. Cover it with lining to match the rest of the box.

• Set the false bottom on top of the glued strips. To flip it up, press down in the middle of the side without strip supports.

51

DECOR: INTRODUCTION

- A little color and some careful planning can create a terrific-looking room. Become your own decorator and give your room some style that's all your own.

- Before you begin, draw a picture of your room, plan what changes you want to make and color them in with crayons. It's much easier to make changes on a piece of paper than on an entire wall.

- Leftover latex housepaint is your best tool: it's cheap, non-toxic and quick-drying. Brush with it, print with it, squeeze it out of plastic squeeze bottles, or thin it with water and spray it. Warm, soapy water will clean up any paint that's still wet, but once it dries, it's there for good!

- To make decorated surfaces water-proof and washable, coat them with a clear finish such as varnish or clear latex. Even white glue, when diluted with one part water, will protect painted surfaces. Test the glue first, though, to make sure it dries clear.

- Before you begin decorating, trace the position of the furniture in your room with chalk. When you move your furniture out of the way, the chalk marks will be your guidelines. If you plan to paint just one section of a wall, measure and mark the edge with chalk so you'll know where to stop painting. (You can wipe the chalk off later with a damp cloth.)

- Practise painting your patterns, stencils or brush strokes before you begin. Once started, if your design isn't working the way you planned, stop and think. Often you can turn a mistake into a new idea.

- When you paint, work from the top down and from side to side. If you decide to paint an entire wall or add a border around the top of your walls, ask an adult to help you paint the places that are over your head.

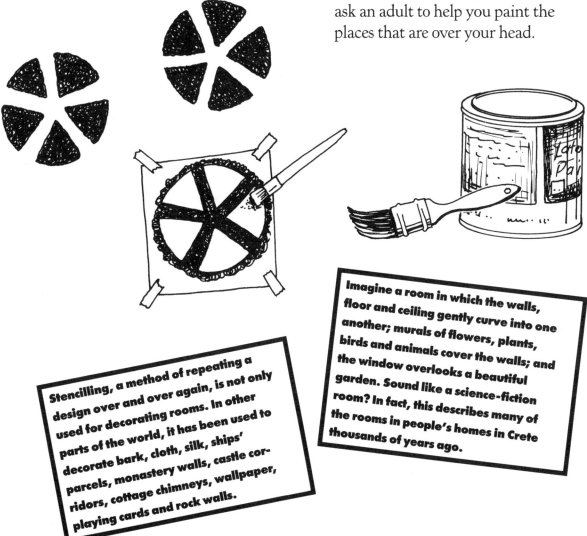

Stencilling, a method of repeating a design over and over again, is not only used for decorating rooms. In other parts of the world, it has been used to decorate bark, cloth, silk, ships' parcels, monastery walls, castle corridors, cottage chimneys, wallpaper, playing cards and rock walls.

Imagine a room in which the walls, floor and ceiling gently curve into one another; murals of flowers, plants, birds and animals cover the walls; and the window overlooks a beautiful garden. Sound like a science-fiction room? In fact, this describes many of the rooms in people's homes in Crete thousands of years ago.

SPONGE-PAINTED WALLS

Dab the walls of your room with a painted sponge to create a great new look.

- **MATERIALS**
  - *latex paint* • *rubber gloves* • *newsprint (or scrap paper)* • *water* • *chalk*
  - *ruler* • *newspaper* • *shallow containers (plates or lids)* • *large sponge (natural or synthetic)*

- **PREPARATION**
  - Decide if you will paint a whole wall, just one section, just the top half or just the bottom half. Use chalk and a ruler to mark where you want the sponging to end.

  - Ask someone to help you move your furniture out of the way. Cover the whole floor area with newspaper. Wear old clothes and rubber gloves.

  - Choose a paint color that suits the color already on your wall. (The present color will show through.) Soft, pastel shades work well together. Thin your paint with a little water for an even softer look.

  - Practise sponging some news-print to get the desired effect before sponging your wall. If you want sponge marks that are less regular in shape, tear bits off the edges of the sponge.

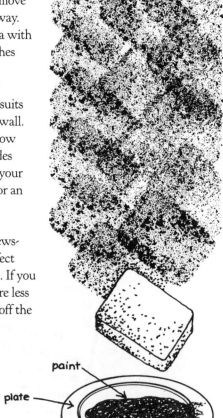

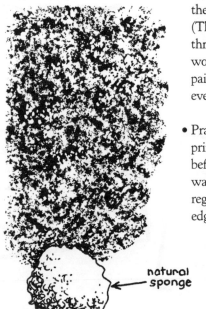

natural sponge

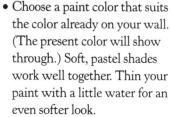

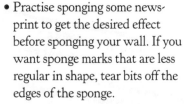

paint

plate

54

- **INSTRUCTIONS**

1. Wet your sponge and wring it out to soften it. Pour some paint into a shallow container.

2. Dip one side of the sponge lightly into the paint. Don't soak up too much paint or it will drip down the wall.

3. Dab the sponge onto one spot. Lift the sponge and dab on another spot. Overlap the paint "dabs" to get an even pattern all over. Repeat, dipping the sponge in the paint as necessary.

4. Continue dabbing until you have covered the whole area. Stand back and look at the wall. Add a few dabs to any areas that look less painted.

5. Clean your sponge and work area with warm, soapy water as soon as you've finished, before the paint has a chance to dry.

- **VARIATION 1**

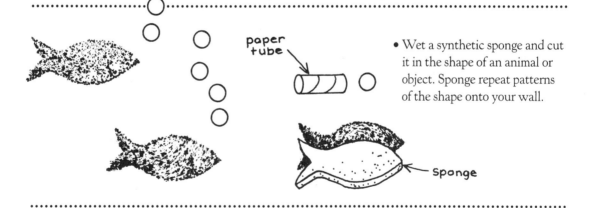

paper tube

sponge

- Wet a synthetic sponge and cut it in the shape of an animal or object. Sponge repeat patterns of the shape onto your wall.

- **VARIATION 2**

- For a different effect try "ragging." Bunch up a soft rag in your hand, dip it into some paint, and dab it onto the wall. Also try covering a twisted rag with paint and rolling it down the wall. Practise first on paper.

STENCILLED BORDER

Design a stencil to print colorful borders
on your walls and accents on your furniture.

● **MATERIALS**
• *paper and pencil* • *sharp scissors* • *10 inch x 10 inch square of clear plastic (container lid or vinyl)
or thin cardboard* • *masking tape* • *acrylic, latex or tempera paint* • *plate or lid* • *small sponge
or brush with short bristles* • *newspaper* • *pad of damp newspaper*

● **PREPARATION**

• Plan a simple design on paper. It
can be one shape or a combina-
tion of simple shapes. Cut out
your design and trace the outline
onto the clear plastic.

• Carefully cut out the inside of
the shape with small, sharp
scissors to make a stencil. Trim
the outside edges of the stencil so
that only about an inch remains
around the cut-out design.

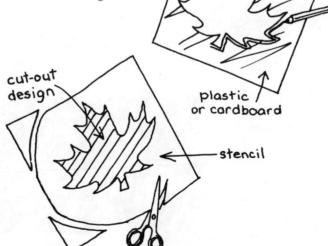

pencil
line

paper

paper
pattern

plastic
or cardboard

cut-out
design

stencil

• If you decide to paint a straight
border, use chalk and a ruler to
draw a guideline for your stencil.

• Put newspaper on the floor
where you will be painting.

• On scrap paper a few layers
thick, practise painting through
the cut-outs in your stencil.

• INSTRUCTIONS

1. Carefully place the stencil on the wall and secure it with several pieces of masking tape.

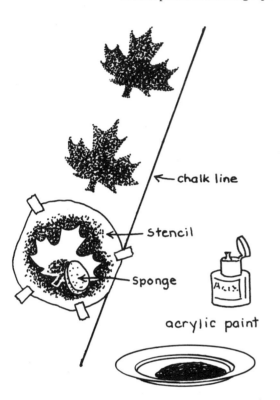

← chalk line

stencil

sponge

acrylic paint

2. Pour some paint into a plate or lid. Dab very small amounts of paint onto your sponge or brush. Gently pat the paint in the cut-out areas of the stencil. If you overload your sponge with paint, the paint will leak under the edge of the stencil.

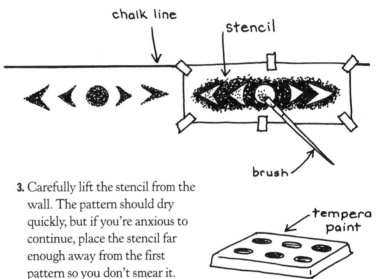

chalk line

stencil

brush

tempera paint

3. Carefully lift the stencil from the wall. The pattern should dry quickly, but if you're anxious to continue, place the stencil far enough away from the first pattern so you don't smear it.

4. Continue moving the stencil and painting until the design is complete.

5. While you move the stencil, rest your sponge or brush on a pad of damp newspapers to keep it moist.

• VARIATION

• Accordion-fold a 2½-foot strip of waxed paper. Cut out a simple pattern on one side. Unfold and flatten the waxed paper.

waxed paper

• Hold the waxed-paper stencil in place with pieces of masking tape and paint inside the shapes. You may need to replace the stencil with a new one if it wears out before your border is finished.

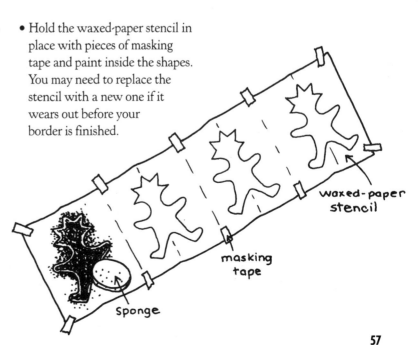

waxed-paper stencil

masking tape

sponge

WALL DOODLE

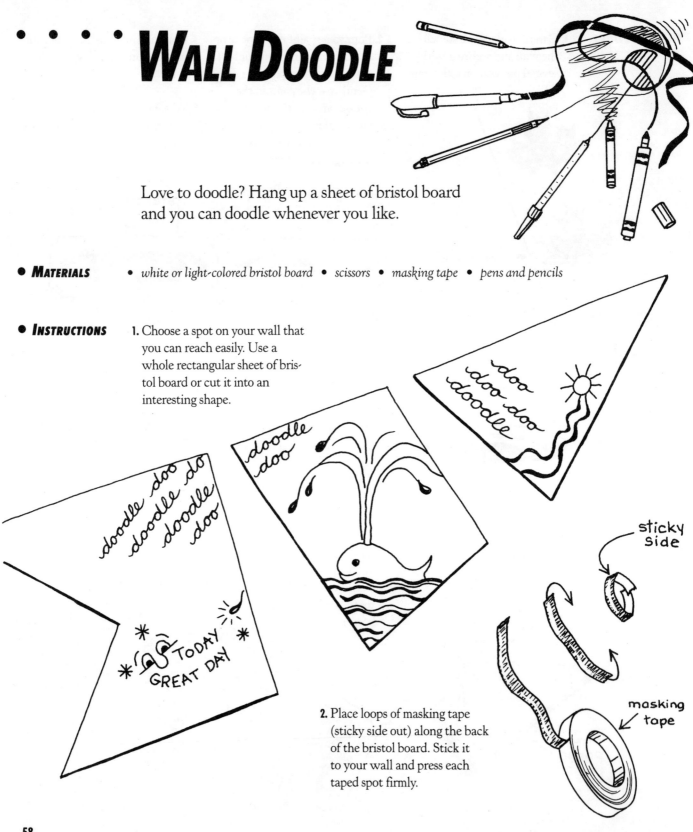

Love to doodle? Hang up a sheet of bristol board
and you can doodle whenever you like.

● **MATERIALS**   • *white or light-colored bristol board* • *scissors* • *masking tape* • *pens and pencils*

● **INSTRUCTIONS**   1. Choose a spot on your wall that
you can reach easily. Use a
whole rectangular sheet of bristol board or cut it into an
interesting shape.

doodle doo do
doodle do doo
doodle
doo

TODAY
GREAT DAY

doodle
doo

doo
doo doo
doodle

sticky
side

masking
tape

2. Place loops of masking tape
(sticky side out) along the back
of the bristol board. Stick it
to your wall and press each
taped spot firmly.

58

3. Keep a container of pens and pencils nearby so you can cover your doodle board with drawings, scribbles, squiggles and autographs. Doodle each time the mood strikes – it makes a great diary.

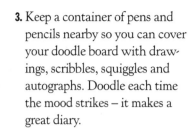
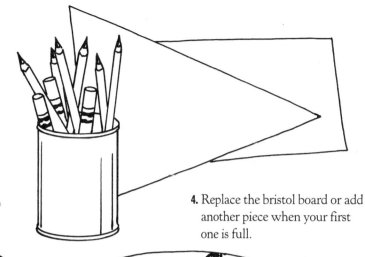

4. Replace the bristol board or add another piece when your first one is full.

● **VARIATION 1**

• Make a doodle board with a personal touch. Attach a photograph of yourself to your wall with masking tape. Cut a piece of bristol board in the shape of a cartoon speech balloon. Tape it to the wall next to your photo.

photo

what I would really like to say...

bristol board

● **VARIATION 2**

• Hang a long strip of heavy, white paper on the wall. Use tempera paints, crayons, pencils, or colored paper and glue to create a mural.

STARLIGHT

Create a glow-in-the-dark constellation
on your wall and sleep under the stars every night.

- **MATERIALS**
  - chalk • non-toxic clear luminous paint, or neon paint, or glow-in-the-dark paint (from a craft store) • paintbrush

- **PREPARATION**
  - Look in an astronomy book or study the night sky to plan your real or imaginary star constellations. Notice that some constellations have both large and small stars.

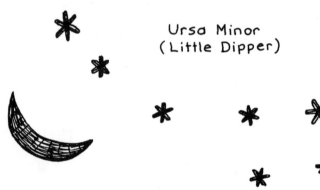

Ursa Minor
(Little Dipper)

Cassiopeia

Cepheus

  - To decide where to paint your stars, lie on your bed and look around. Choose a wall beside or across from your bed or a piece of furniture or a lampshade.

- **INSTRUCTIONS**
  1. With chalk, lightly map out your constellation. Draw a 3-inch circle for each large star and a 2-inch circle for each smaller one.

  2. Paint a star shape inside each circle. Three lines crossed over at the center work well.

chalk line

  3. You may need to apply several coats of paint. If you use clear paint, it will be almost invisible in daylight.

  4. When the paint is dry, gently rub away the chalk lines with a damp rag.

- **VARIATION 1**

  - Remove your light-switch plate from the wall and place it on some newspaper.

  - Paint stars or patterns on the plate with neon or glow-in-the-dark paints to make it glow at night. Let dry and screw it back in place.

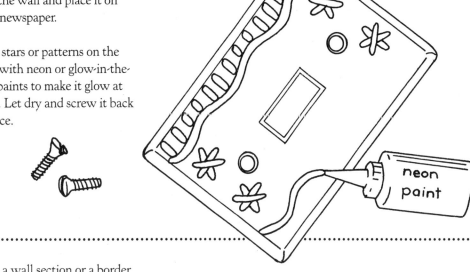

- **VARIATION 2**

  - Paint a wall section or a border around the top of your room with dark blue, latex paint. Let it dry and then add some glittery star stickers to create another kind of constellation.

DOOR DECOR

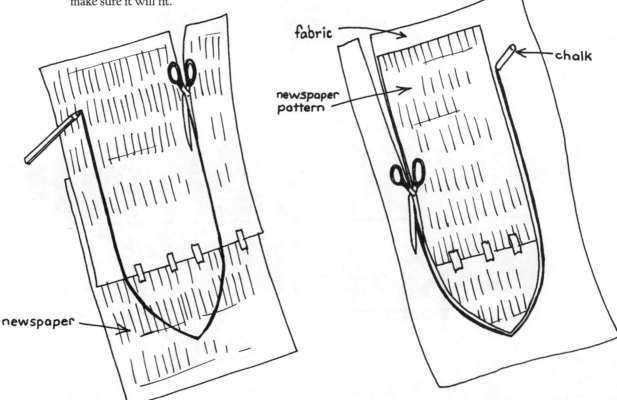

Make a huge one-of-a-kind banner to dress up your door.

- **MATERIALS**
  - newspaper • pencil • scissors • chalk • large piece of felt or other fabric
  - decorations (buttons, ribbon, fabric scraps, fabric paints and markers) • white glue
  - heavy cardboard • heavy string or fishing line • flat thumbtacks

- **INSTRUCTIONS**

  1. Make a large newspaper pattern of the banner shown here. Hold it up to your door to make sure it will fit.

  2. Use chalk to trace the paper pattern onto your large piece of fabric. Cut the banner out.

fabric

chalk

newspaper pattern

newspaper

3. Decorate your banner by gluing on fabric scraps, ribbon and buttons, or by using fabric paints or markers. Add a pocket for messages. Leave 2 inches at the top of the banner undecorated.

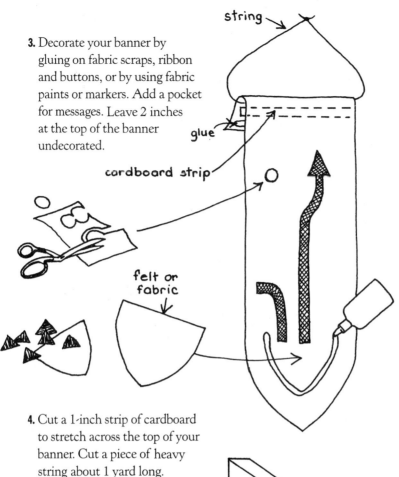

string

glue

cardboard strip

felt or fabric

4. Cut a 1-inch strip of cardboard to stretch across the top of your banner. Cut a piece of heavy string about 1 yard long.

. . . .

5. Lay your banner face down. Place the cardboard strip on the banner 2 inches from the top. Center the string on the cardboard strip. Apply a thick band of glue to the top 2 inches of the banner. Flip over the glued fabric and press down firmly. Let dry.

6. Tie the ends of the string together. Push two thumbtacks halfway into the top of your door about 8 inches apart. Hang the string around the thumbtacks.

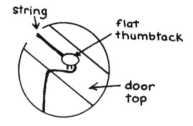

string

flat thumbtack

door top

7. Center your banner on the two tacks. Then push the tacks securely into the door to hold your banner straight.

. . . .

• **VARIATION**

• For a festive occasion, wrap up your door, or someone else's, like an enormous gift. Cover the outside of the door in cheerful paper or fabric. Cut and glue together wide strips of brightly colored plastic, fabric or crepe paper to make one very long piece or four shorter pieces of ribbon.

• Wrap the very long ribbon around the door from the outside to the inside. Cross the fabric, bring the ends back to the outside and tie in a bow.

Becky

• Or, on the inside of the door, attach one of the four pieces of ribbon at the top, one at the bottom, and one on either side, with tacks. Bring the ribbon pieces around to the outside of the door and tie the ends in a huge bow.

• Cut a large gift tag from heavy paper, decorate it and attach it to the bow.

BEAUTIFUL BLINDS

Add some pizzazz to a plain window blind and brighten your day.

● **MATERIALS**
- vinyl, pull-down window blind • paper and pencil • chalk • indelible markers, fabric markers, latex paint or fabric paint • paintbrushes or squeeze bottles (optional) • stencil (optional)

● **PREPARATION**
- Carefully plan the design for your blind on paper.
- Cover your work area with newspaper.

● **INSTRUCTIONS**

1. Unroll the window blind completely and lay it flat on a table or the floor so that the side that will face into your room faces up.

chalk

2. Lightly sketch your design onto the blind with chalk. You can remove any visible chalk when you're done by rubbing gently with a soft rag.

3. Decorate your blind with paint or markers according to your design. Or use paint and a stencil for a repeating design. (See "Stencilled Border" on page 56.)

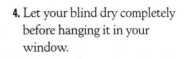

4. Let your blind dry completely before hanging it in your window.

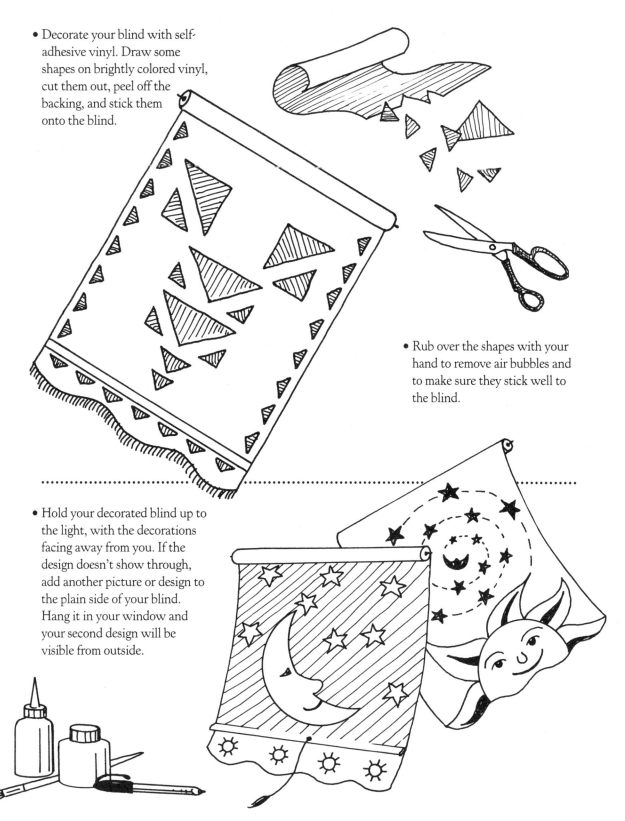

- **VARIATION 1**
  - Decorate your blind with self-adhesive vinyl. Draw some shapes on brightly colored vinyl, cut them out, peel off the backing, and stick them onto the blind.

  - Rub over the shapes with your hand to remove air bubbles and to make sure they stick well to the blind.

- **VARIATION 2**
  - Hold your decorated blind up to the light, with the decorations facing away from you. If the design doesn't show through, add another picture or design to the plain side of your blind. Hang it in your window and your second design will be visible from outside.

DESIGNER SHEETS

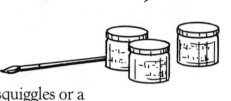

Paint flowers, dinosaurs, spatters, squiggles or a favorite design on your sheets and pillowcases.

● **MATERIALS**
- pre-washed white or light-colored bedsheet and pillowcase • fabric scrap • chalk
- newspaper • fabric paint • paintbrushes, plastic squeeze bottles or sponge

● **PREPARATION**
- Get permission to paint your sheets.

- Paint a scrap of fabric with your fabric paint. If it stiffens the fabric when dry, use it only on the borders of your sheet and pillowcase.

- Mix yellow, red and blue (the primary colors) to make any secondary colors you would like to use (orange, purple and green). Add white to colors to make pastel shades.

- Cover the floor with several layers of newspaper and spread your sheet out on the newspaper.

● **INSTRUCTIONS**
1. Lightly sketch your design on the sheet with chalk. These lines will wash out later.

2. Paint your design onto the sheet and pillowcase. Use a large paintbrush for broad strokes and large dabs. Add details with a smaller paintbrush. Use a sponge to dab on a soft, textured paint pattern.

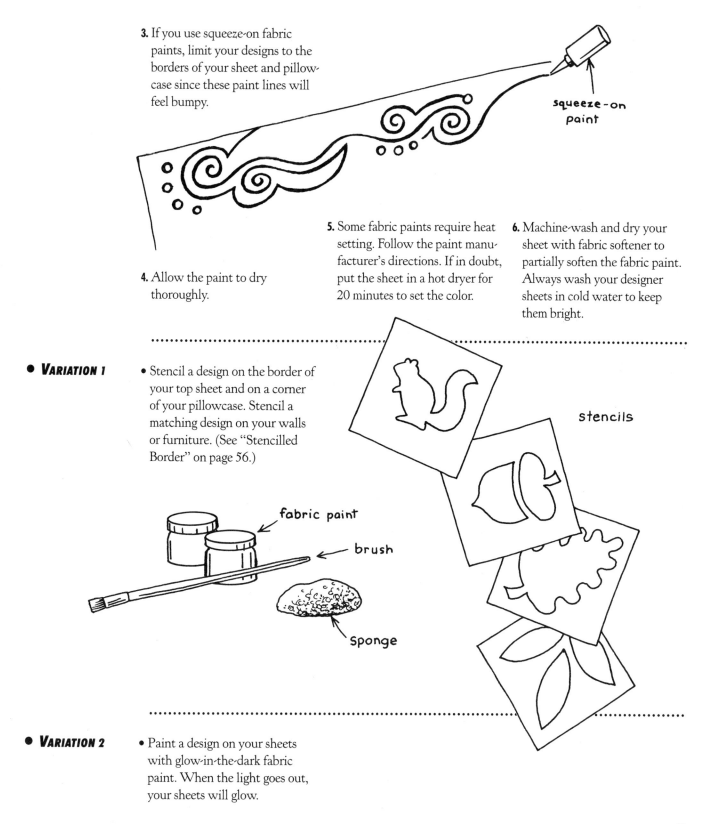

3. If you use squeeze-on fabric paints, limit your designs to the borders of your sheet and pillowcase since these paint lines will feel bumpy.

squeeze-on paint

4. Allow the paint to dry thoroughly.

5. Some fabric paints require heat setting. Follow the paint manufacturer's directions. If in doubt, put the sheet in a hot dryer for 20 minutes to set the color.

6. Machine-wash and dry your sheet with fabric softener to partially soften the fabric paint. Always wash your designer sheets in cold water to keep them bright.

• **VARIATION 1**

• Stencil a design on the border of your top sheet and on a corner of your pillowcase. Stencil a matching design on your walls or furniture. (See "Stencilled Border" on page 56.)

stencils

fabric paint

brush

Sponge

• **VARIATION 2**

• Paint a design on your sheets with glow-in-the-dark fabric paint. When the light goes out, your sheets will glow.

TIE-DYED SHEETS

With a little fabric paint, you can make dazzling tie-dyed sheets. Just gather, twist and spray.

● **MATERIALS**
- *white or light-colored bedsheet and pillowcase* • *brightly colored acrylic or water-based fabric paints* • *clean spray bottles* • *newspaper* • *large elastic bands or string*

● **PREPARATION**

- Get permission to dye your sheets. If they are new, wash them to remove sizing (starch that prevents paint from penetrating).

- In a clean spray bottle, mix one part fabric paint to four or more parts water. Shake to make a watery dye. Pour the dye into a clean spray bottle. Use a separate bottle for each color.

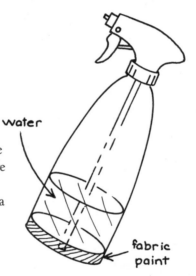

water

fabric paint

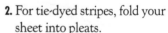

- For a muted effect, dampen your sheets before you paint them. The colors will bleed slightly, creating a softer look. Spraying dry sheets gives a crisper look.

- Cover your work surface with several layers of newspaper and wear old clothes.

● **INSTRUCTIONS**

1. For a spiral tie-dye, lay the sheet flat on a table or the floor. Grasp a handful of fabric at the center and turn it around and around until the sheet forms a circular mound.

2. For tie-dyed stripes, fold your sheet into pleats.

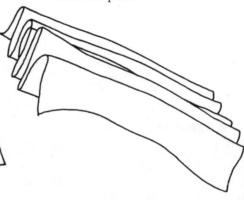

3. For tie-dyed circles, take one handful of sheet at a time and wrap it with an elastic band or string.

4. Spray one or more colors onto the arranged sheet, covering it with lots of color. Carefully open the sheet. If you want more color, rearrange your sheet and spray it again. Carefully open it once more and hang it to dry.

5. Clean each spray bottle and nozzle well with soapy water as soon as you have finished with it.

6. Some fabric paints require heat setting. Follow the paint manu-facturer's directions. If in doubt, toss the sheet in a hot dryer for 20 minutes to set the color. Always wash your tie-dyed sheets in cold water to keep them bright.

7. If your sheet seems a little stiff, wait a few days. Then wash it in cold water and dry it using fabric softener.

 VARIATION

• Tie-dye another sheet or a length of plain fabric using the same technique, and hang it as a matching curtain.

COMFORTER COVER

Make a classy cover for your comforter (or sleeping bag) and turn it into a work of art.

● **MATERIALS**
- *2 plain, flat sheets* • *chalk* • *large scissors* • *newspaper* • *paintbrush or plastic squeeze bottle or spray bottle or sponge* • *fabric paint* • *needle and thread*

● **PREPARATION**
- Cover your work surface with newspaper.

- Read the sections on making tie-dyed and designer sheets, and choose the painting methods you would like to use. (See "Tie-Dyed Sheets" on page 68 and "Designer Sheets" on page 66.)

- Get permission to paint the two sheets. If they are new, wash them first to remove the starch.

● **INSTRUCTIONS**

1. Spread out both sheets, one on top of the other. Lay your open sleeping bag or your comforter on top. Make a chalk line 2 inches out from the edge of the comforter. Cut along the chalk line.

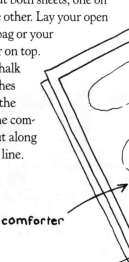

comforter

sheets

chalk

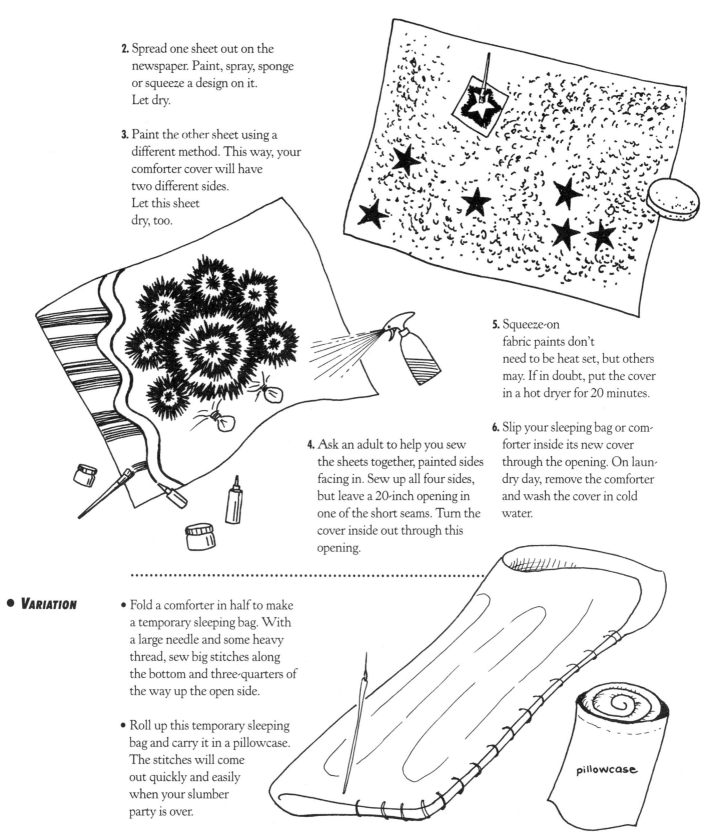

2. Spread one sheet out on the newspaper. Paint, spray, sponge or squeeze a design on it. Let dry.

3. Paint the other sheet using a different method. This way, your comforter cover will have two different sides. Let this sheet dry, too.

4. Ask an adult to help you sew the sheets together, painted sides facing in. Sew up all four sides, but leave a 20-inch opening in one of the short seams. Turn the cover inside out through this opening.

5. Squeeze-on fabric paints don't need to be heat set, but others may. If in doubt, put the cover in a hot dryer for 20 minutes.

6. Slip your sleeping bag or comforter inside its new cover through the opening. On laundry day, remove the comforter and wash the cover in cold water.

• **VARIATION**

• Fold a comforter in half to make a temporary sleeping bag. With a large needle and some heavy thread, sew big stitches along the bottom and three-quarters of the way up the open side.

• Roll up this temporary sleeping bag and carry it in a pillowcase. The stitches will come out quickly and easily when your slumber party is over.

pillowcase

EXTRAS: INTRODUCTION

- Even if your room looks great, a few extras can add some zip. All you need is a little spare time and some materials from around the house: scissors, white glue, paper, paint, plastic, fabric and string. You might need some aluminum cans or flour and salt from the kitchen, and perhaps you'll want to buy some plexiglass.

- Use bits and pieces of your family's favorite old clothing to create a fabric collage full of memories. Raid the rag bag for a little piece of that old shirt you liked so much, a sleeve from your brother's favorite pajamas, and so on. Old, worn-out clothing can be recycled and used in lots of crafts.

- Love to draw or write? Treat your art with pride. Display your favorite drawings and poems in frames you've made yourself. They're simple to make, but they add special meaning to your art and give your room extra personality.

- If you like to hang a lot of artwork, posters or decorations on your walls, ask an adult to help you hang a picture rail. Just fasten some wood trimming to a wall horizontally at eye level. The picture rail will put an end to pin holes, nail holes and tape marks on your walls.

- Once your room is decorated just as you like, you're ready for visitors. They'll know they are welcome when they read the message on your doorknob dial. And to let you know they have arrived, your guests can ring your homemade, personalized doorbells.

Not long ago in the 1930s, the first mobiles, made of wire and colored balls, were invented. These balls and other shapes moved about with the help of a motor. Today, most mobiles are made with string and flat shapes that catch the wind and spin, creating different effects.

Among art professionals, paintings are considered more beautiful when they are properly displayed in frames. Old paintings are often set in elaborately carved wood and gold frames. Modern drawings, paintings and collages, however, are usually displayed in simple, straight-edged, metal or wood frames.

DOORKNOB DIAL

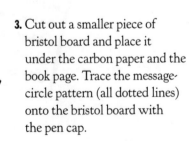

Use this decorative message dial to tell the world when you're in and when you're not.

● **MATERIALS**
- carbon paper (or paper and pencil) • scissors • white bristol board • pen cap or other blunt, pointed object • colored markers or pencils • metal paper fastener

● **PREPARATION**
- If you don't have any carbon paper, make your own by rubbing the side of an ordinary graphite pencil all over one side of a piece of paper.

● **INSTRUCTIONS**

1. Cut a piece of white bristol board the same size as this book page.

2. Place it under the pattern on page 75. Place a piece of carbon paper (shiny side down) between the book page and the bristol board. With the point of a pen cap, trace over all the solid lines in the door-hanger pattern. Remove the bristol board.

carbon paper face down

bristol board

3. Cut out a smaller piece of bristol board and place it under the carbon paper and the book page. Trace the message-circle pattern (all dotted lines) onto the bristol board with the pen cap.

4. Cut the door-hanger and the message circle from the bristol board. Color them and write your messages.

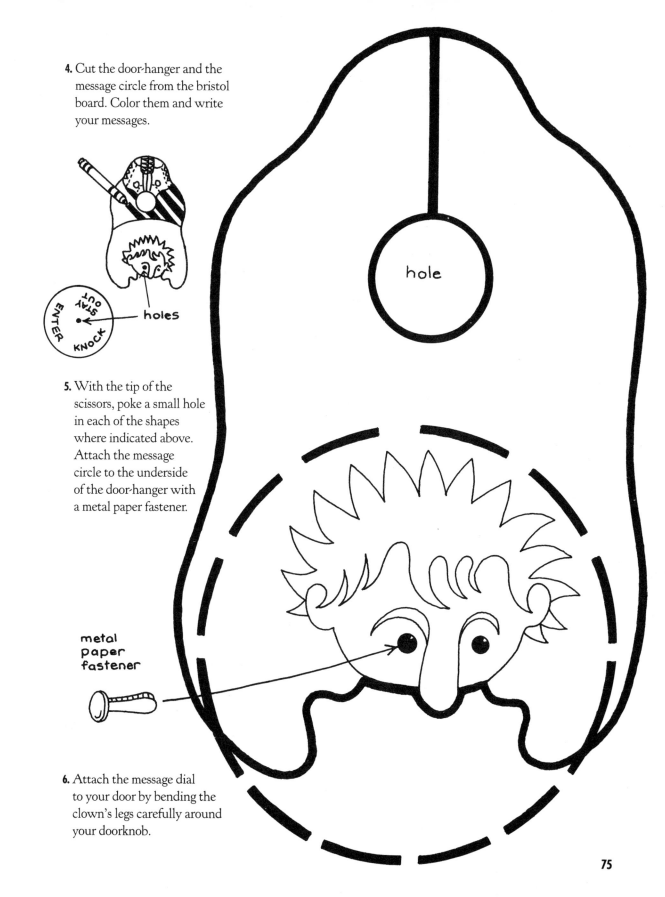

holes

ENTER KNOCK STAY OUT

hole

5. With the tip of the scissors, poke a small hole in each of the shapes where indicated above. Attach the message circle to the underside of the door-hanger with a metal paper fastener.

metal paper fastener

6. Attach the message dial to your door by bending the clown's legs carefully around your doorknob.

75

Fabric Family

Make a collage of memories from bits of your family's worn-out favorite clothes.

- **Materials**
  - fabric scraps • bristol board • scissors • white glue • paintbrush • pencil • paper
  - decorations (buttons, sequins and yarn) • pen or marker • dowel, string and finishing nails

- **Preparation**
  - Gather as much of your family's worn-out clothing, rags and fabric scraps as you can find.
  - Decide which fabric you will use to represent each person in your fabric family.

- **Instructions**

1. Cut light-colored fabric pieces and arrange them on the bristol board to form a background. Trim them to make them fit.

2. Remove the fabric pieces, but remember where each goes. Paint the entire surface of the bristol board with a thin coat of glue. Carefully place each piece of your fabric background on top of the bristol board. Rub gently to remove air bubbles.

3. Draw a paper pattern for each person you'd like to represent on your collage. Cut out all of your patterns.

4. Trace each pattern piece onto a brightly colored fabric scrap. You can make each person's clothing from one piece or several pieces of fabric. Trace heads and hands onto flesh-colored fabric.

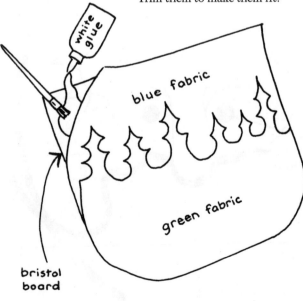

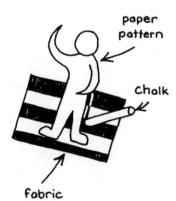

5. Cut out the fabric pieces and arrange them on the fabric background, spacing out your characters evenly.

6. Glue the fabric shapes on one at a time. Add buttons, sequins and bits of yarn for hair. Use a pen or marker to add facial features.

7. Make loops from other fabric scraps and glue them along the top edge of your collage. Let dry. Slide a dowel through the loops and ask an adult to hang it using string or a few finishing nails.

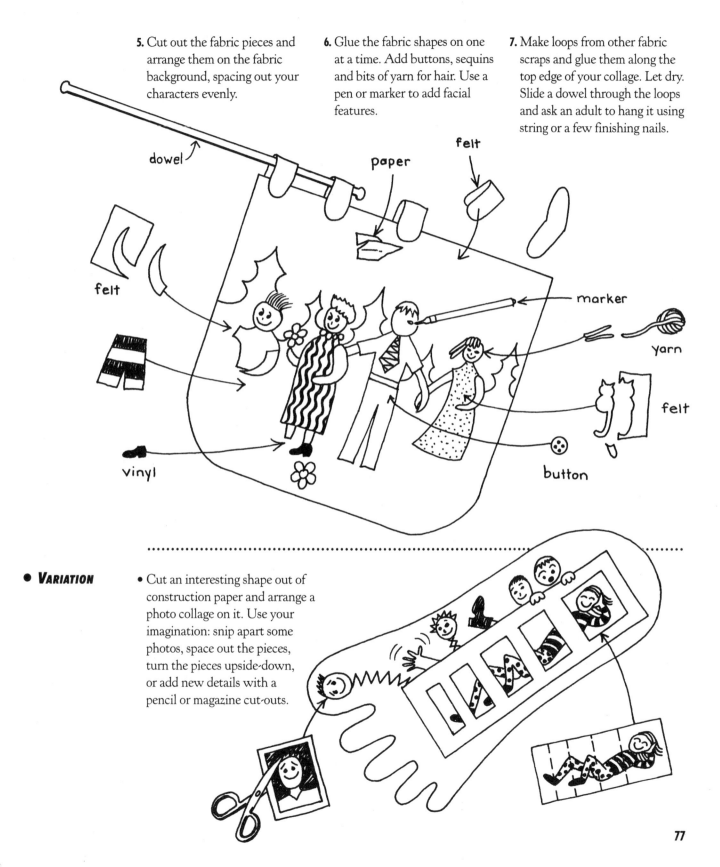

dowel

felt

vinyl

paper

felt

button

marker

yarn

felt

- **VARIATION**

- Cut an interesting shape out of construction paper and arrange a photo collage on it. Use your imagination: snip apart some photos, space out the pieces, turn the pieces upside-down, or add new details with a pencil or magazine cut-outs.

FLEXY FRAME

Assemble a great-looking picture frame and display a different masterpiece each week.

- **MATERIALS**
  - 12-inch square plexiglass • 12-inch square bristol board • ruler • pencil • 12 inches heavy string
  - masking tape • decorative tape, 1½ inches wide (from a hardware store) • 2 thumbtacks or a nail

- **PREPARATION**
  - Have a piece of plexiglass cut to the appropriate size at a hardware, lumber or art supply store.
  - Cut a piece of bristol board the same size.

- **INSTRUCTIONS**

1. On the right and left edges of the bristol-board square, make a mark 4 inches down from the top. Line up your ruler along these marks, and make two dots 4 inches apart near the center of the ruler. Punch a hole through each dot.

2. Thread 1 foot of sturdy string through the two holes and knot the ends together. Stick masking tape over the holes and along the string on one side of the bristol board.

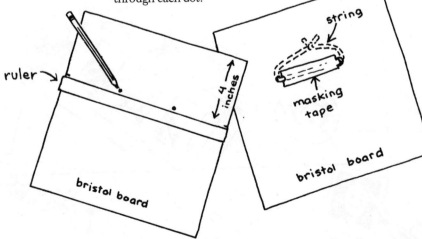

3. Cut a 1-foot piece of decorative tape and fold it evenly over the top edge of the plexiglass square.

4. Lay the bristol-board square tape side up and lay the plexiglass on top. Line up the edges.

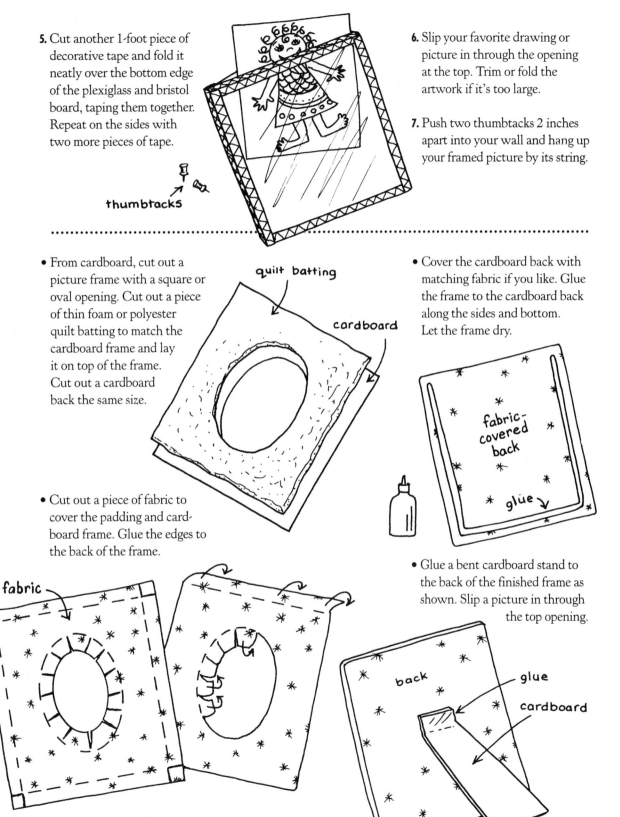

5. Cut another 1-foot piece of decorative tape and fold it neatly over the bottom edge of the plexiglass and bristol board, taping them together. Repeat on the sides with two more pieces of tape.

thumbtacks

6. Slip your favorite drawing or picture in through the opening at the top. Trim or fold the artwork if it's too large.

7. Push two thumbtacks 2 inches apart into your wall and hang up your framed picture by its string.

● **VARIATION**

• From cardboard, cut out a picture frame with a square or oval opening. Cut out a piece of thin foam or polyester quilt batting to match the cardboard frame and lay it on top of the frame. Cut out a cardboard back the same size.

quilt batting

cardboard

• Cut out a piece of fabric to cover the padding and cardboard frame. Glue the edges to the back of the frame.

fabric

• Cover the cardboard back with matching fabric if you like. Glue the frame to the cardboard back along the sides and bottom. Let the frame dry.

fabric-covered back

glue

• Glue a bent cardboard stand to the back of the finished frame as shown. Slip a picture in through the top opening.

back

glue

cardboard

79

PAPIER-MÂCHÉ FRAME

Make a three-dimensional frame for your favorite drawing or photo.

● **MATERIALS**
- *newspaper* • *bowl* • *cardboard* • *scissors* • *5 inches string* • *1 cup water*
- *1 cup flour* • *⅓ cup salt* • *paint and paintbrush* • *masking tape* • *small nail*

● **PREPARATION**

- Choose a drawing or photo that you would like to design a special frame to hold.

- Tear newspaper into ½ inch x ½ inch pieces and soak 3 cups in a bowl of water overnight. The next day, drain and squeeze out the excess water, leaving the pulp moist.

● **INSTRUCTIONS**

1. Cut a cardboard frame big enough to fit around your drawing or photo.

2. Poke two small holes in the top edge of the cardboard frame and tie a loop of string through them. This will be your picture hanger.

3. Add 1 cup water, 1 cup flour and ⅓ cup salt to the moist newspaper pulp. Mix it well and knead it until the mush has an even consistency.

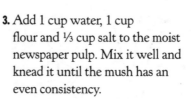

string loop

cardboard

1 cup water

1 cup flour

salt

papier-mâché mush

4. Place small handfuls of this mush onto the cardboard frame to cover it. Mold the mush; add bumps and push down dents as part of your design.

5. Let the mush dry completely, and then paint over it.

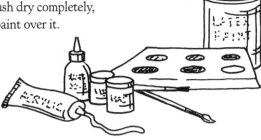

6. Use masking tape to fasten your picture to the back of the frame. Trim off the corners if necessary. Hang your picture on the wall with a small nail.

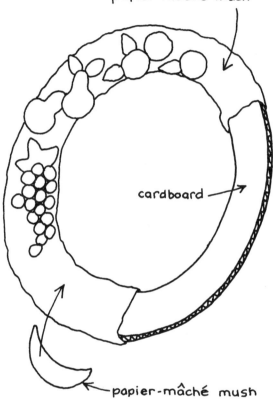

papier-mâché mush

cardboard

papier-mâché mush

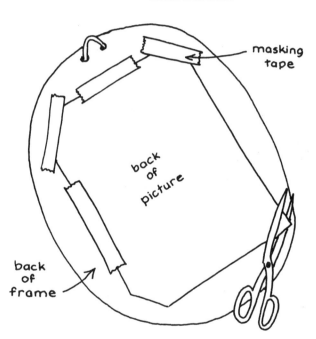

masking tape

back of picture

back of frame

• **VARIATION**

• Make a note holder. Lay a paper tube on its side. Cut a slit across the top half. Use papier-mâché mush to add feet, a head and a tail. Let it dry and paint it. Slip a note or a greeting card into the slit at the top.

Have a Great Day

MOBILE OF FRIENDS

Make a mobile of friendly characters that dance and change whenever a breeze stirs.

- **MATERIALS**
  - photos • magazine or catalogue pictures • colored markers or pencils (optional) • scissors
  - glue • lightweight cardboard • needle and thread • plastic lid (6-8 inches wide)

- **INSTRUCTIONS**

1. Cut out eight heads, all about the same size, from photos, magazines or catalogues. Then cut out eight bodies and eight pair of feet as well. If you can't find enough pictures, draw and color some yourself.

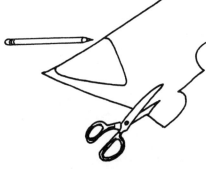

2. Glue four of the heads onto cardboard, leaving some space in between them. Cut out each one and glue a head on the other side. Do the same with the bodies and feet, so that you have four head pieces, four body pieces and four feet pieces, each with a picture on the front and back.

3. Group the heads, bodies and feet to make four characters. Sew the body parts of each character together with a needle and thread, leaving a ½-inch gap between body parts.

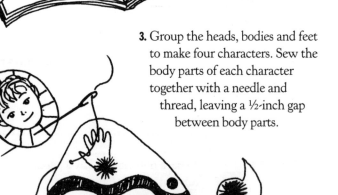

4. Cut the inner circle out of a plastic lid. Suspend the four cardboard characters from the rim of the lid with thread, spacing them apart evenly.

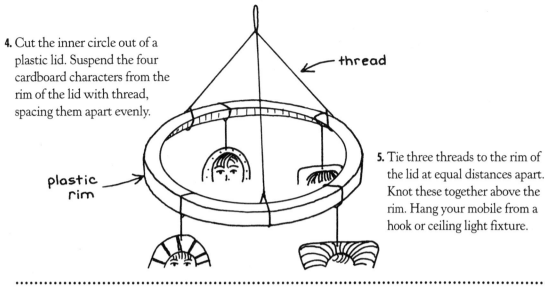

thread

plastic rim

5. Tie three threads to the rim of the lid at equal distances apart. Knot these together above the rim. Hang your mobile from a hook or ceiling light fixture.

- **VARIATION**

- Fold some 2-inch squares of brightly colored paper as shown, and cut them into snowflakes.

fold

fold

- Cut out some 3-inch circles of clear, self-adhesive vinyl. Peel the backing from one of the circles and stick a paper snowflake on it, color side down. Repeat this with another snowflake, then stick the two circles together, snowflake to snowflake.

- Make several more snowflake pairs and tie them to a lid with thread as described above. Hang your snowflake mobile in a window.

sticky sides together

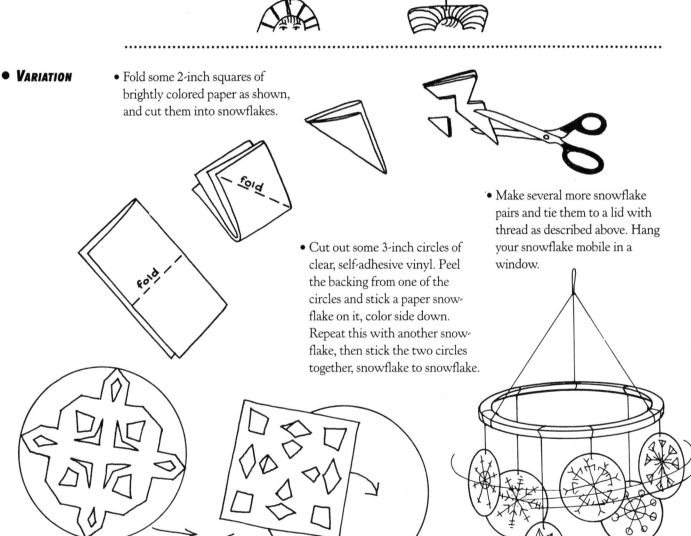

83

AIR ACROBAT

Design a lightweight acrobat to hang over an air vent. When the air comes on, your acrobat will dance.

● **MATERIALS**
- paper and pencil • plastic shopping bag • scissors • clear tape
- waterproof markers • needle • 10 feet thread • thumbtack

● **INSTRUCTIONS**

1. On paper, draw and cut out a body shape like the one shown here. It should be about 8 inches high and 8 inches wide. Trace it onto the plastic bag twice and cut out.

2. Lay the plastic body shapes on a flat surface and tape a strip of paper ½ inch x 8 inches along the bottom edge of each.

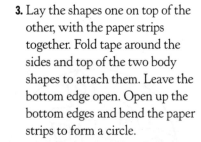

plastic

paper strip

tape

3. Lay the shapes one on top of the other, with the paper strips together. Fold tape around the sides and top of the two body shapes to attach them. Leave the bottom edge open. Open up the bottom edges and bend the paper strips to form a circle.

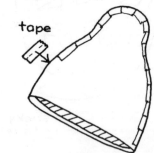

tape

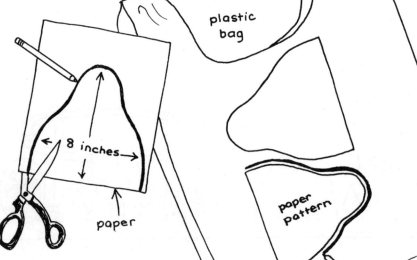

plastic bag

8 inches

paper

paper pattern

4. Cut two 1 inch x 12 inch plastic strips for arms, and tape them onto the body. Add thin plastic strips for hair.

5. For legs, cut two 1 inch x 18 inch strips of plastic. Sew through the top of each leg, up between the paper strips into the body, and out through the top of the head.

6. Use waterproof markers to add features to your acrobat.

7. With a thumbtack, attach the thread to the ceiling or window-sill above an open air vent. When the air blows out, watch your acrobat dance.

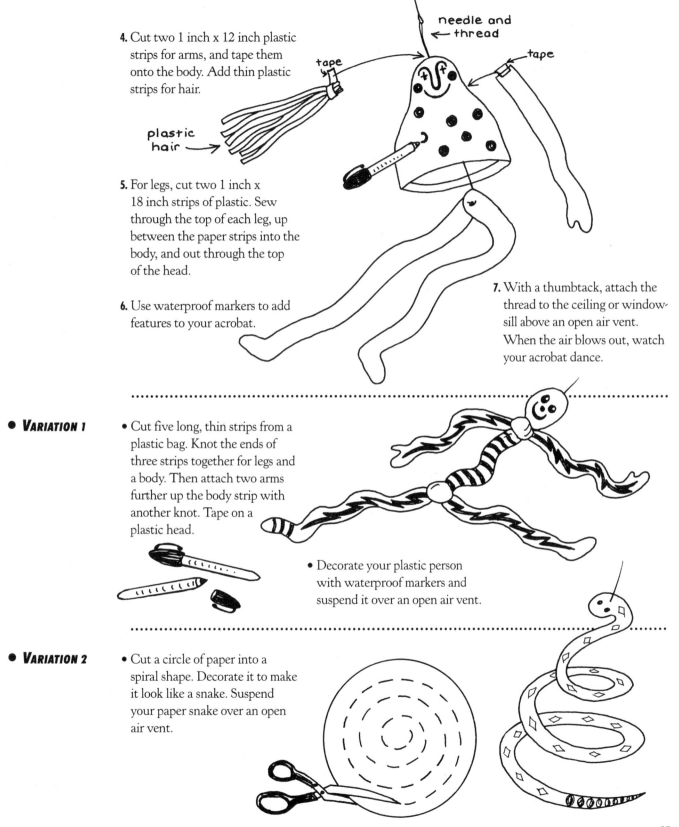

- **VARIATION 1**
  - Cut five long, thin strips from a plastic bag. Knot the ends of three strips together for legs and a body. Then attach two arms further up the body strip with another knot. Tape on a plastic head.

  - Decorate your plastic person with waterproof markers and suspend it over an open air vent.

- **VARIATION 2**
  - Cut a circle of paper into a spiral shape. Decorate it to make it look like a snake. Suspend your paper snake over an open air vent.

DING-DONG DOORBELLS

You can turn some old cans, washers, nuts and bolts into a set of doorbells for your room.

● **MATERIALS**
- aluminum cans • block of wood (to fit inside cans) • hammer and nail
- metal file or thick tape • washers, nuts, large beads or buttons
- heavy string, ribbon or yarn • 5 feet ribbon • thumbtacks
- decorations (paint, self-adhesive vinyl, fabric scraps)

● **PREPARATION**
- Remove the label from each can and clean them thoroughly.

- Have an adult place each can over the block of wood and, with a nail, hammer a hole in the bottom. File off any sharp edges on the cans or cover them with thick tape.

nail

hammer

can

wood block

● **INSTRUCTIONS**
1. Tie a nut, washer, button or bead to the end of a piece of heavy string, ribbon or yarn. Slip on a few more. This will be the clapper that goes inside the bell.

knot

2. Tie a loose knot in the string a few inches up from the last bead. Thread the long end of the string up into the can and out through the hole punched in the bottom.

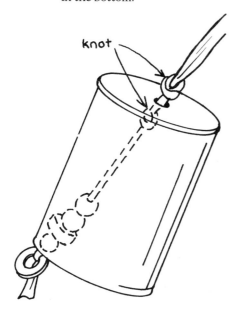

knot

3. Adjust the loose knot in the string so that the clapper knocks against the bottom rim of the upside-down can.

4. To hold the clapper in place, tie another knot in the string directly above the can.

5. Make more can bells, varying their size and shape as well as what you use for the clappers and string.

6. Decorate the outside of each can with squeeze-on paints, self-adhesive vinyl cut-outs, scraps of felt or paper. The decorations may change the sound of the doorbell.

flat thumbtacks

top of door

← ribbon

knot

paint

handle

7. Use flat thumbtacks to fasten one end of a 5-foot ribbon to the top edge of the door. Tie the bells to the ribbon at different levels. Use the bottom part of the ribbon as a doorbell handle or tie on a large ring. Visitors can shake the handle to let you know they've arrived.

INDEX